LOST DORSAI

ACE SCIENCE FICTION BOOKS
NEW YORK

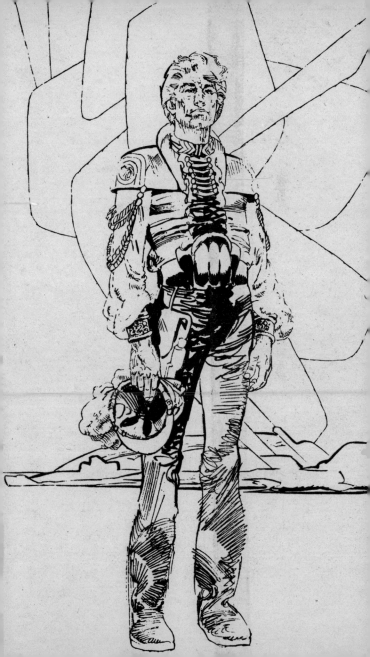

Ace Science Fiction Books by Gordon R. Dickson

ALIEN ART & ARCTURUS LANDING
THE ALIEN WAY
THE FAR CALL
HOME FROM THE SHORES
IN IRON YEARS
LOVE NOT HUMAN
MASTERS OF EVERON
NAKED TO THE STARS
ON THE RUN
THE SPACE SWIMMERS
SPACEPAW
SPACIAL DELIVERY
TIME TO TELEPORT/DELUSION WORLD

The *Childe Cycle* Series

NECROMANCER
TACTICS OF MISTAKE
DORSAI!
SOLDIER, ASK NOT
LOST DORSAI
SPIRIT OF DORSAI
THE FINAL ENCYCLOPEDIA (coming in November '85)

LOST DORSAI

GORDON R. DICKSON

Afterword by Sandra Miesel
Illustrations by Fernando

A shorter version of this work appeared in *Destinies,* Vol. II, no. 1;
February-March 1980, copyright © 1980 by Charter Communications, Inc.
The story "Warrior" first appeared in *Analog,* copyright © 1965 by Condé
Nast Publications, Inc.

LOST DORSAI

An Ace Science Fiction Book / published by arrangement with
the author

PRINTING HISTORY
Ace trade edition / August 1980
Ace mass market edition / October 1981
Sixth printing / April 1985

ISBN: 0-441-49302-5

Ace Science Fiction Books are published by The Berkley Publishing Group,
200 Madison Avenue, New York, New York 10016.
PRINTED IN THE UNITED STATES OF AMERICA

LOST DORSAI

I am Corunna El Man.

I brought the little courier vessel down at last at the spaceport of Nahar City on Ceta, the large world around Tau Ceti. I had made it from the Dorsai in six phase shifts to transport, to the stronghold of Gebel Nahar, our Amanda Morgan—she whom they call the Second Amanda.

Normally I am far too senior in rank to act as a courier pilot. But I had been home on leave at the time. The courier vessels owned by the Dorsai Cantons are too expensive to risk lightly, but the situation required a contracts expert at Nahar more swiftly than one could safety be gotten there. They had asked me to take on the problem, and I had solved it by stretching the possibilities on each of the phase shifts, coming here.

The risks I had taken had not seemed to bother Amanda. That was not surprising, since she was Dorsai. But neither did she talk to me much on the trip; and that was a thing that had come to be, with me, a little unusual.

For things had been different for me after Baunpore. In the massacre there following the siege, when the North Freilanders finally overran the town, they cut up my face for the revenge of it; and they killed Else, for no other reason than that she was my wife. There was nothing left of her then but incandescent gas, dissipating throughout the universe; and since there could be no hope of a grave, nothing to come back to, nor any place where she could be remembered, I rejected surgery then, and chose to wear my scars as a memorial to her.

It was a decision I never regretted. But it was true that with those scars came an alteration in the way other people reacted to me. With some I found that I became almost invisible; and nearly all seemed to relax their natural impulse to keep private their personal secrets and concerns.

It was almost as if they felt that somehow I was now beyond the point where I would stand in judgment on their pains and sorrows. No, on second thought, it was something even stronger than that. It was as if I was like a burnt-out candle in the dark room of their inner selves—a lightless, but safe, companion whose presence reassured them that their privacy was still unbreached. I doubt very much that Amanda and those I was to meet on this trip to Gebel Nahar would have talked to me as freely as they later did, if I had met them back in the days when I had had Else, alive.

We were lucky on our incoming. The Gebel Nahar is more a mountain fortress than a palace or government center; and for military reasons Nahar City, near it, has a spaceport capable of handling deep-space ships. We debarked, expecting to be met in the terminal the minute we entered it through its field doors. But we were not.

The principality of Nahar Colony lies in tropical latitudes on Ceta, and the main lobby of the terminal was small, but high-ceilinged and airy; its floor and ceiling tiled in bright colors, with plants growing in planter areas all about; and bright, enormous, heavily-framed paintings on all the walls. We stood in the

middle of all this and foot traffic moved past and around us. No one looked directly at us, although neither I with my scars, nor Amanda—who bore a remarkable resemblance to those pictures of the first Amanda in our Dorsai history books—were easy to ignore.

I went over to check with the message desk and found nothing there for us. Coming back, I had to hunt for Amanda, who had stepped away from where I had left her.

"El Man—" her voice said without warning, behind me. "Look!"

Her tone had warned me, even as I turned. I caught sight of her and the painting she was looking at, all in the same moment. It was high up on one of the walls; and she stood just below it, gazing up.

Sunlight through the transparent front wall of the terminal flooded her and the picture, alike. She was in all the natural colors of life—as Else had been—tall, slim, in light blue cloth jacket and short cream-colored skirt, with white-blond hair and that incredible youthfulness that her namesake ancestor had also owned. In contrast, the painting was rich in garish pigments, gold leaf and alizarin crimson, the human figures it depicted caught in exaggerated, melodramatic attitudes.

Leto de muerte, the large brass plate below it read. *Hero's Death-Couch*, as the title would roughly translate from the bastard, archaic Spanish spoken by the Naharese. It showed a great, golden bed set out on an open plain in the aftermath of the battle. All about were corpses and bandaged officers standing in gilt-encrusted uniforms. The living surrounded the bed and its occupant, the dead Hero, who, powerfully muscled yet emaciated, hideously wounded and stripped to the waist, lay upon a thick pile of velvet cloaks, jewelled weapons, marvellously-wrought tapestries and golden utensils, all of which covered the bed.

The body lay on its back, chin pointing at the sky, face gaunt with the agony of death, still firmly holding by one large hand to its naked chest, the hilt of an oversized and ornate sword, its massive blade darkened with blood. The wounded officers standing about and gazing at the corpse were posed in dramatic attitudes. In the foreground, on the earth beside the bed, a single ordinary soldier in battle-torn uniform, dying, stretched forth one arm in tribute to the dead man.

Amanda looked at me for a second as I moved up beside her. She did not say anything. It was not necessary to say anything. In order to live, for two hundred years we on the Dorsai have exported the only commodity we owned—the lives of our generations—to be spent in wars for others' causes. We live with real war; and to those who do that, a painting like this one was close to obscenity.

"So that's how they think here," said Amanda.

I looked sideways and down at her. Along with the appearance of her ancestor, she had inherited the First Amanda's incredible youthfulness. Even I, who knew she was only a half-dozen years younger than myself— and I was now in my mid-thirties—occasionally forgot that fact, and was jolted by the realization that she thought like my generation rather than like the stripling she seemed to be.

"Every culture has its own fantasies," I said. "And

this culture's Hispanic, at least in heritage."

"Less than ten percent of the Naharese population's Hispanic nowadays, I understand," she answered. "Besides, this is a caricature of Hispanic attitudes."

She was right. Nahar had originally been colonized by immigrants—Gallegos from the northwest of Spain who had dreamed of large ranches in a large open Territory. Instead, Nahar, squeezed by its more industrial and affluent neighbors, had become a crowded, small country which had retained a bastard version of the Spanish language as its native tongue and a medley of half-remembered Spanish attitudes and customs as its culture. After the first wave of immigrants, those who came to settle here were of anything but Hispanic ancestry, but still they had adopted the language and ways they found here.

The original ranchers had become enormously rich —for though Ceta was a sparsely populated planet, it was food-poor. The later arrivals swelled the cities of Nahar, and stayed poor—very poor.

"I hope the people I'm to talk to are going to have more than ten per cent of ordinary sense," Amanda said. "This picture makes me wonder if they don't prefer fantasy. If that's the way it is at Gebel Nahar. . ."

She left the sentence unfinished, shook her head, and then—apparently pushing the picture from her mind—smiled at me. The smile lit up her face, in something more than the usual sense of that phrase. With her, it was something different, an inward lighting deeper and greater than those words usually indicate. I had only met her for the first time, three days earlier, and Else was all I had ever or would ever want; but now I could see what people had meant on the

Dorsai, when they had said she inherited the first Amanda's abilities to both command others and make them love her.

"No message for us?" she said.

"No—" I began. But then I turned, for out of the corner of my eye I had seen someone approaching us.

She also turned. Our attention had been caught because the man striding toward us on long legs was a Dorsai. He was big. Not the size of the Graeme twins, Ian and Kensie, who were in command at Gebel Nahar on the Naharese contract; but close to that size and noticeably larger than I was. However, Dorsai come in all shapes and sizes. What had identified him to us—and obviously, us to him—was not his size but a multitude of small signals, too subtle to be catalogued. He wore a Naharese army bandmaster's uniform, with warrant officer tabs at the collar; and he was blond-haired, lean-faced, and no more than in his early twenties. I recognized him.

. He was the third son of a neighbor from my own canton of High Island, on the Dorsai. His name was Michael de Sandoval, and little had been heard of him for six years.

"Sir—Ma'm," he said, stopping in front of us. "Sorry to keep you waiting. There was a problem getting transport."

"Michael," I said. "Have you met Amanda Morgan?"

"No, I haven't." He turned to her. "An honor to meet you, ma'm. I suppose you're tired of having everyone say they recognize you from your great-grandmother's pictures?"

"Never tire of it," said Amanda cheerfully; and gave

him her hand. "But you already know Corunna El Man?"

"The El Man family are High Island neighbors," said Michael. He smiled for a second, almost sadly, at me. "I remember the Captain from when I was only six years old and he was first home on leave. If you'll come along with me, please? I've already got your luggage in the bus."

"Bus?" I said, as we followed him toward one of the window-wall exits from the terminal.

"The band bus for Third Regiment. It was all I could get."

We emerged on to a small parking pad scattered with a number of atmosphere flyers and ground vehicles. Michael de Sandoval led us to a stubby-framed, powered lifting body, that looked as if it could hold about thirty passengers. Inside, one person saved the vehicle from being completely empty. It was an Exotic in a dark blue robe, an Exotic with white hair and a strangely ageless face. He could have been anywhere between thirty and eighty years of age and he was seated in the lounge area at the front of the bus, just before the compartment wall that divided off the control area in the vehicle's nose. He stood up as we came in.

"Padma, Outbond to Ceta," said Michael. "Sir, may I introduce Amanda Morgan, Contracts Adjuster, and Corunna El Man, Senior Ship Captain, both from the Dorsai? Captain El Man just brought the Adjuster in by courier."

"Of course, I know about their coming," said Padma.

He did not offer a hand to either of us. Nor did he

rise. But, like many of the advanced Exotics I have known, he did not seem to need to. As with those others, there was a warmth and peace about him that the rest of us were immediately caught up in, and any behavior on his part seemed natural and expected.

We sat down together. Michael ducked into the control compartment, and a moment later, with a soft vibration, the bus lifted from the parking pad.

"It's an honor to meet you, Outbond," said Amanda. "But it's even more of an honor to have you meet us. What rates us that sort of attention?"

Padma smiled slightly.

"I'm afraid I didn't come just to meet you," he said to her. "Although Kensie Graeme's been telling me all about you; and—" he looked over at me, "even I've heard of Corunna El Man."

"Is there anything you Exotics don't hear about?" I said.

"Many things," he shook his head, gently but seriously.

"What was the other reason that brought you to the spaceport, then?" Amanda asked.

He looked at her thoughtfully.

"Something that has nothing to do with your coming," he said. "It happens I had a call to make to elsewhere on the planet, and the phones at Gebel Nahar are not as private as I liked. When I heard Michael was coming to get you, I rode along to make my call from the terminal, here."

"It wasn't a call on behalf of the Conde of Nahar, then?" I asked.

"If it was—or if it was for anyone but myself—" he smiled. "I wouldn't want to betray a confidence by admitting it. I take it you know about El Conde? The titular ruler of Nahar?"

"I've been briefing myself on the Colony and on Gebel Nahar ever since it turned out I needed to come here," Amanda answered.

I could see her signalling me to leave her alone with him. It showed in the way she sat and the angle at which she held her head. Exotics were perceptive, but I doubted that Padma had picked up that subtle private message.

"Excuse me," I told them. "I think I'll go have a word with Michael."

I got up and went through the door into the control section, closing it behind me. Michael sat relaxed, one hand on the control rod; and I sat down myself in the copilot's seat.

"How are things at home, sir?" he asked, without turning his head from the sky ahead of us.

"I've only been back this once since you'd have left, yourself," I said. "But it hasn't changed much. My father died last year."

"I'm sorry to hear that."

"Your father and mother are well—and I hear your brothers are all right, out among the stars," I said. "But, of course, you know that."

"No," he said, still watching the sky ahead. "I haven't heard for quite a while."

A silence threatened.

"How did you happen to end up here?" I asked. It was almost a ritual question between Dorsais away from home.

"I heard about Nahar. I thought I'd take a look at it."

"Did you know it was as fake Hispanic as it is?"

"Not fake," he said. "Something . . . but not that."

He was right, of course.

"Yes," I said, "I guess I shouldn't use the word fake. Situations like the one here come out of natural causes, like all others."

He looked directly at me. I had learned to read such looks since Else died. He was very close in that moment to telling me something more than he would probably have told anyone else. But the moment passed and he looked back out the windshield.

"You know the situation here?" he said.

"No. That's Amanda's job," I said. "I'm just a driver on this trip. Why don't you fill me in?"

"You must know some of it already," he said, "and Ian or Kensie Graeme will be telling you the rest. But in any case . . . the Conde's a figurehead. Literally. His father was set up with that title by the first Naharese immigrants, who're all now rich ranchers. They had a dream of starting their own hereditary aristocracy here, but that never really worked. Still, on paper, the Conde's the hereditary sovereign of Nahar; and, in theory, the army belongs to him as Commander-in-Chief. But the army's always been drawn from the poor of Nahar—the city poor and the *campesinos;* and they hate the rich first-immigrants. Now there's a revolution brewing and the army doesn't know which way it'll jump."

"I see," I said. "So a violent change of government is on the way, and our contract here's with a government which may be out of power tomorrow. Amanda's got a problem."

"It's everyone's problem," Michael said. "The only

reason the army hasn't declared itself for the revolutionaries is because its parts don't work together too well. Coming from the outside, the way you have, the ridiculousness of the locals' attitudes may be what catches your notice first. But actually those attitudes

are all the non-rich have, here, outside of a bare existence—this business of the flags, the uniforms, the music, the duels over one wrong glance and the idea of dying for your regiment—or being ready to go at the throat of any other regiment at the drop of a hat."

"But," I said, "what you're describing isn't any practical, working sort of military force."

"No. That's why Kensie and Ian were contracted in here, to do something about turning the local army into something like an actual defensive force. The other principalities around Nahar all have their eyes on the ranchlands, here. Given a normal situation, the Graemes'd already be making progress—you know Ian's reputation for training troops. But the way it's turned out, the common soldiers here think of the Graemes as tools of the ranchers, the revolutionaries preach that they ought to be thrown out, and the regiments are non-cooperating with them. I don't think they've got a hope of doing anything useful with the army under present conditions; and the situation's been getting more dangerous daily—for them, and now for you and Amanda, as well. The truth is, I think Kensie and Ian'd be wise to take their loss on the contract and get out."

"If accepting loss and leaving was all there was to it, someone like Amanda wouldn't be needed here," I said. "There has to be more than that to involve the Dorsai in general."

He said nothing.

"How about you?" I said. "What's your position here? You're Dorsai too."

"Am I?" he said to the windshield, in a low voice.

I had at last touched on what had been going unspoken between us. There was a name for individuals like Michael, back home. They were called "lost Dorsai." The name was not used for those who had chosen to do something other than a military vocation. It was reserved for those of Dorsai heritage who seemed to have chosen their life work, whatever it was, and then—suddenly and without explanation—abandoned it. In Michael's case, as I knew, he had graduated from the Academy with honors; but after graduation he had abruptly withdrawn his name from assignment and left the planet, with no explanation, even to his family.

"I'm Bandmaster of the Third Naharese Regiment," he said, now. "My regiment likes me. The local people don't class me with the rest of you, generally—" he smiled a little sadly, again, "except that I don't get challenged to duels."

"I see," I said.

"Yes." He looked over at me now. "So, while the army is still technically obedient to the Conde, as its Commander-in-Chief, actually just about everything's come to a halt. That's why I had trouble getting transportation from the vehicle pool to pick you up."

"I see—" I repeated. I had been about to ask him some more; but just then the door to the control compartment opened behind us and Amanda stepped in.

"Well, Corunna," she said, "how about giving me a chance to talk with Michael?"

She smiled past me at him; and he smiled back. I did not think he had been strongly taken by her—whatever was hidden in him was a barrier to anything like that. But her very presence, with all it implied of home, was plainly warming to him.

"Go ahead," I said, getting up. "I'll go say a word or two to the Outbond."

"He's worth talking to," Amanda spoke after me as I went.

I stepped out, closed the door behind me, and rejoined Padma in the lounge area. He was looking out the window beside him and down at the plains area that lay between the town and the small mountain from which Gebel Nahar took its name. The city we had just left was on a small rise west of that mountain, with suburban and planted areas in between. Around and beyond that mountain—for the fort-like residence that was Gebel Nahar faced east—the actual, open grazing land of the cattle plains began. Our bus was one of those vehicles designed to fly ordinarily at about tree-top level, though of course it could go right up to the limits of the atmosphere in a pinch, but right now we were about three hundred meters up. As I stepped out of the control compartment, Padma took his attention from the window and looked back at me.

"Your Amanda's amazing," he said, as I sat down facing him, "for someone so young."

"She said something like that about you," I told him. "But in her case, she's not quite as young as she looks."

"I know," Padma smiled. "I was speaking from the viewpoint of my own age. To me, even you seem young."

I laughed. What I had had of youth had been far back, some years before Baunpore. But it was true that in terms of years I was not even middle-aged.

"Michael's been telling me that a revolution seems to be brewing here in Nahar," I said to him.

"Yes." He sobered.

"That wouldn't be what brings someone like you to Gebel Nahar?"

His hazel eyes were suddenly amused.

"I thought Amanda was the one with the questions," he said.

"Are you surprised I ask?" I said. "This is an out of the way location for the Outbond to a full planet."

"True." He shook his head. "But the reasons that bring me here are Exotic ones. Which means, I'm afraid, that I'm not free to discuss them."

"But you know about the local movement toward a revolution?"

"Oh, yes." He sat in perfectly relaxed stillness, his hands loosely together in the lap of his robe, light brown against the dark blue. His face was calm and unreadable. "It's part of the overall pattern of events on this world."

"Just this world?"

He smiled back at me.

"Of course," he said gently, "our Exotic science of ontogenetics deals with the interaction of all known human and natural forces, on all the inhabited worlds. But the situation here in Nahar, and specifically the situation at Gebel Nahar, is primarily a result of local, Cetan forces."

"International planetary politics."

"Yes," he said. "Nahar is surrounded by five other principalities, none of which have cattle-raising land like this. They'd all like to have a part or all of this Colony in their control."

"Which ones are backing the revolutionaries?"

He gazed out the window for a moment without

speaking. It was a presumptuous thought on my part to imagine that my strange geas, that made people want to tell me private things, would work on an Exotic. But for a moment I had had the familiar feeling that he was about to open up to me.

"My apologies," he said at last. "It may be that in my old age I'm falling into the habit of treating everyone else like—children."

"How old are you, then?"

He smiled.

"Old—and getting older."

"In any case," I said, "you don't have to apologize to me. It'll be an unusual situation when bordering countries don't take sides in a neighbor's revolution."

"Of course," he said. "Actually, all of the five think they have a hand in it on the side of the revolutionaries. Bad as Nahar is, now, it would be a shambles after a successful revolution, with everybody fighting everybody else for different goals. The other principalities all look for a situation in which they can move in and gain. But you're quite right. International politics is always at work, and it's never simple."

"What's fueling this situation, then?"

"William," Padma looked directly at me and for the first time I felt the remarkable effect of his hazel eyes. His face held such a calmness that all his expression seemed to be concentrated in those eyes.

"William?" I asked.

"William of Ceta."

"That's right," I said, remembering. "He owns this world, doesn't he?"

"It's not really correct to say he owns it," Padma said. "He controls most of it—and a great many parts of other worlds. Our present-day version of a merchant prince, in many ways. But he doesn't control everything, even here on Ceta. For example, the Naharese ranchers have always banded together tightly to deal with him; and his best efforts to split them apart and gain a direct authority in Nahar, haven't worked. He controls after a fashion, but only by manipulating the outside conditions that the ranchers have to deal with."

"So he's the one behind the revolution?"

"Yes."

It was plain enough to me that it was William's involvement here that had brought Padma to this backwater section of the planet. The Exotic science of ontogenetics, which was essentially a study of how humans interacted, both as individuals and societies, was something they took very seriously; and William, as one of the movers and shakers of our time would always have his machinations closely watched by them.

"Well, it's nothing to do with us, at any rate," I said, "except as it affects the Graeme's contract."

"Not entirely," he said. "William, like most gifted individuals, knows the advantage of killing two, or even fifty, birds with one stone. He hires a good many mercenaries, directly and indirectly. It would benefit him if events here could lower the Dorsai reputation and the market value of its military individuals."

"I see—" I began; and broke off as the hull of the bus rang suddenly—as if to a sharp blow.

"Down!" I said, pulling Padma to the floor of the vehicle and away from the window beside which we had been sitting. One good thing about Exotics—they trust you to know your own line of work. He obeyed me instantly and without protest. We waited . . . but there was no repetition of the sound.

"What was it?" he asked, after a moment, but without moving from where I had brought him.

"Solid projectile slug. Probably from a heavy hand weapon," I told him. "We've been shot at. Stay down, if you please, Outbond."

I got up myself, staying low and to the center of the bus, and went through the door into the control compartment. Amanda and Michael both looked around at me as I entered, their faces alert.

"Who's out to get us?" I asked Michael.

He shook his head.

"I don't know," he said. "Here in Nahar, it could be anything or anybody. It could be the revolutionaries or simply someone who doesn't like the Dorsai; or someone who doesn't like Exotics—or even someone who doesn't like me. Finally, it could be someone drunk, drugged, or just in a macho mood."

"—who also has a military hand weapon."

"There's that," Michael said. "But everyone in Nahar is armed; and most of them, legitimately or not, own military weapons."

He nodded at the windscreen.

"Anyway, we're almost down," he said.

I looked out. The interlocked mass of buildings that was the government seat called Gebel Nahar was sprawled halfway down from the top of the small mountain, just below us. In the tropical sunlight, it looked like a resort hotel, built on terraces that descended the steep slope. The only difference was that each terrace terminated in a wall, and the lowest of the

walls were ramparts of solid fortifications, with heavy weapons emplaced along them. Gebel Nahar, properly garrisoned, should have been able to dominate the countryside against surface troops all the way out to the horizon, at least on this side of the mountain.

"What's the other side like?" I asked.

"Mountaineering cliff—there's heavy weapon emplacements cut out of the rock there, too, and reached by tunnels going clear through the mountain," Michael answered. "The ranchers spared no expense when they built this place. Gallego thinking. They and their families might all have to hole up here, one day."

But a few moments later we were on the poured concrete surface of a vehicle pool. The three of us went back into the body of the bus to rejoin Padma; and Michael let us out of the vehicle. Outside, the parking area was abnormally silent.

"I don't know what's happened—" said Michael as we set foot outside. We three Dorsai had checked, instinctively, ready to retreat back into the bus and take off again if necessary.

A voice shouting from somewhere beyond the ranked flyers and surface vehicles, brought our heads around. There was the sound of running feet, and a moment later a soldier wearing an energy sidearm, but dressed in the green and red Naharese army uniform with band tabs, burst into sight and slid to a halt, panting before us.

"Sir—" he wheezed, in the local dialect of archaic Spanish. "Gone—"

We waited for him to get his breath; after a second, he tried again.

"They've deserted, sir!" he said to Michael, trying to pull himself to attention. "They've gone—all the regiments, everybody!"

"When?" asked Michael.

"Two hours past. It was all planned. Certainly, it was planned. In each group, at the same time, a man stood up. He said that now was the time to desert, to show the *ricones* where the army stood. They all marched out, with their flags, their guns, everything. Look!"

He turned and pointed. We looked. The vehicle pool was on the fifth or sixth level down from the top of the Gebel Nahar. It was possible to see, from this as from any of the other levels, straight out for miles over the plains. Looking now we saw, so far off no other sign was visible, the tiny, occasional twinkles of reflected sunlight, seemingly right on the horizon.

"They are camped out there; waiting for an army they say will come from all the other countries around, to reinforce them and accomplish the revolution."

"Everyone's gone?" Michael's words in Spanish brought the soldier's eyes back to him.

"All but us. The soldiers of your band, sir. We are the Conde's Elite Guard, now."

"Where are the two Dorsai Commanders?"

"In their offices, sir."

"I'll have to go to them right away," said Michael to the rest of us. "Outbond, will you wait in your quarters, or will you come along with us?"

"I'll come," said Padma.

The five of us went across the parking area, between the crowded vehicles and into a maze of corridors. Through these at last we found our way finally to a

large suite of offices, where the outward wall of each room was all window. Through the window of the one we were in, we looked out on the plain below, where the distant and all but invisible Naharese regiments were now camped. We found Kensie and Ian Graeme together in one of the inner offices, standing talking before a massive desk large enough to serve as a conference table for a half-dozen people.

They turned as we came in—and once again I was hit by the curious illusion that I usually experienced on meeting these two. It was striking enough whenever I approached one of them. But when the twins were together, as now, the effect was enhanced.

In my own mind I had always laid it to the fact that in spite of their size—and either one is nearly a head taller than I am—they are so evenly proportioned physically that their true dimensions do not register on you until you have something to measure them by. From a distance it is easy to take them for not much more than ordinary height. Then, having unconsciously underestimated them, you or someone else whose size you know approaches them; and it is that individual who seems to change in size as he, or she, or you get close. If it is you, you are very aware of the change. But if it is someone else, you can still seem to shrink somewhat, along with that other person. To feel yourself become smaller in relationship to someone else is .a strange sensation, if the phenomenon is entirely subjective.

In this case, the measuring element turned out to be Amanda, who ran to the two brothers the minute we entered the room. Her home, Fal Morgan, was the homestead closest to the Graeme home of Foralie and the three of them had grown up together. As I said, she was not a small woman, but by the time she had reached them and was hugging Kensie, she seemed to have become not only tiny, but fragile; and suddenly— again, as it always does—the room seemed to orient itself about the two Graemes.

I followed her and held out my hand to Ian.

"Corunna!" he said. He was one of the few who still called me by the first of my personal names. His large hand wrapped around mine. His face—so different, yet so like, to his twin brother's—looked down into mine. In truth, they were identical, and yet there was all the difference in the universe between them. Only it was not a physical difference, for all its powerful effect on the eye. Literally, it was that Ian was lightless, and all the bright element that might have been in him was instead in his brother, so that Kensie radiated double the human normal amount of sunny warmth. Dark and light. Night and day. Brother and brother.

And yet, there was a closeness, an identity, between them of a kind that I have never seen in any other two human beings.

"Do you have to go back right away?" Ian was asking me. "Or will you be staying to take Amanda back?"

"I can stay," I said. "My leave-time to the Dorsai wasn't that tight. Can I be of use, here?"

"Yes," Ian said. "You and I should talk. Just a minute, though—"

He turned to greet Amanda in his turn and tell Michael to check and see if the Conde was available for a visit. Michael went out with the soldier who had met us at the vehicle pool. It seemed that Michael and

his bandsmen, plus a handful of servants and the Conde himself, added up to the total present population of
Gebel Nahar, outside of those in this room. The ramparts were designed to be defended by a handful of
people, if necessary; but we had barely more than a
handful in the forty members of the regimental band
Michael had led, and they were evidently untrained in
anything but marching.

We left Kensie with Amanda and Padma. Ian led
me into an adjoining office, waved me to a chair, and
took one himself.

"I don't know the situation on your present contract—" he began.

"There's no problem. My contract's to a space force
leased by William of Ceta. I'm leader of Red Flight
under the overall command of Hendrik Galt. Aside
from the fact that Gault would understand, as any other Dorsai would, if a situation like this warranted it,
his forces aren't doing anything at the moment. Which
is why I was on leave in the first place, along with half
his other senior officers. I'm not William's officer. I'm
Gault's."

"Good," said Ian. He turned his head to look past
the high wing of the chair he was sitting in and out
over the plain at where the little flashes of light were
visible. His arms lay relaxed upon the arms of the
chair, his massive hands loosely curved about the ends
of those chair arms. There was, as there always had
been, something utterly lonely but utterly invincible
about Ian. Most non-Dorsais seem to draw a notice-
able comfort from having a Dorsai around in times of
physical danger, as if they assumed that any one of us
would know the right thing to do and so do it. It may

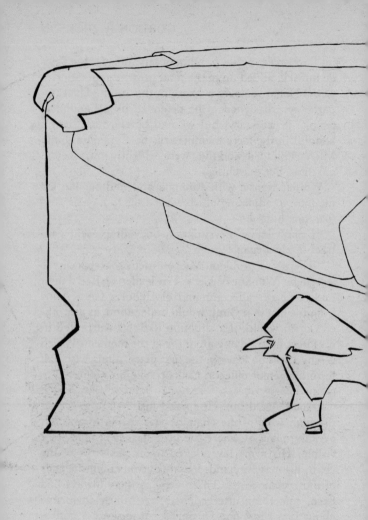

sound fanciful, but I have to say that in somewhat the same way as the non-Dorsai reacted to the Dorsai, so did most of the Dorsai I've known always react to Ian.

But not all of us. Kensie never had, of course. Nor, come to think of it, had any of the other Graemes to my knowledge. But then, there had always been something—not solitary, but independent and apart— about each of the Graemes. Even Kensie. It was a characteristic of the family. Only, Ian had that double share of it.

"It'll take them two days to settle in out there," he said now, nodding at the nearly invisible encampments on the plain. "After that, they'll either have to move against us, or they'll start fighting among themselves. That means we can expect to be overrun here in two days."

"Unless what?" I asked. He looked back at me.

"There's always an unless," I said.

"Unless Amanda can find us an honorable way out of the situation," he said. "As it now stands, there doesn't seem to be any way out. Our only hope is that she can find something in the contract or the situation that the rest of us have overlooked. Drink?"

"Thanks."

He got up and went to a sideboard, poured a couple of glasses half-full of dark brown liquor, and brought them back. He sat down once more, handing a glass to me, and I sniffed at its pungent darkness.

"Dorsai whiskey," I said. "You're provided for, here."

He nodded. We drank.

"Isn't there anything you think she might be able to use?" I asked.

"No," he said. "It's a hope against hope. An honor problem."

"What makes it so sensitive that you need an Adjuster from home?" I asked.

"William. You know him, of course. But how much do you know about the situation here in Nahar?"

I repeated to him what I had picked up from Michael and Padma.

"Nothing else?" he asked.

"I haven't had time to find out anything else. I was asked to bring Amanda here on the spur of the moment, so on the way out I had my hands full. Also, she was busy studying the available data on this situation herself. We didn't talk much."

"William—" he said, putting his glass down on a small table by his chair. "Well, it's my fault we're into this, rather than Kensie's. I'm the strategist, he's the tactician on this contract. The large picture was my job, and I didn't look far enough."

"If there were things the Naharese government didn't tell you when the contract was under discussion, then there's your out, right there."

"Oh, the contract's challengeable, all right," Ian said. He smiled. I know there are those who like to believe that he never smiles; and that notion is nonsense. But his smile is like all the rest of him. "It wasn't the information they held back that's trapped us, it's this matter of honor. Not just our personal honor—the reputation and honor of all Dorsai. They've got us in a position where whether we stay and die or go and live, it'll tarnish the planetary reputation."

I frowned at him.

"How can they do that? How could you get caught

in that sort of trap?"

"Partly," Ian lifted his glass, drank, and put it back down again, "because William's an extremely able strategist himself—again, as you know. Partly, because it didn't occur to me, or Kensie, that we were getting into a three-party rather than a two-party agreement."

"I don't follow you."

"The situation in Nahar," he said, "was always one with its built-in termination clause—I mean, for the ranchers, the original settlers. The type of country they tried to set up was something that could only exist under uncrowded, near-pioneering conditions. The principalities around their grazing area got settled in, some fifty Cetan years ago. After that, the neighboring countries got built up and industrialized; and the semi-feudal notion of open plains and large individual holdings of land got to be impractical, on the international level of this world. Of course, the first settlers, those Gallegos from Galicia in northwest Spain, saw that coming from the start. That was why they built this place we're setting in."

His smile came again.

"But that was back when they were only trying to delay the inevitable," he said. "Sometime in more recent years they evidently decided to come to terms with it."

"Bargain with the more modern principalities around them, you mean?" I said.

"Bargain with the rest of Ceta, in fact," he said. "And the rest of Ceta, nowadays, is William—for all practical purposes."

"There again, if they had an agreement with William that they didn't tell you about," I said, "you've every excuse, in honor as well as on paper, to void the contract. I don't see the difficulty."

"Their deal they've got with William isn't a written, or even a spoken contract," Ian answered. "What the ranchers did was let him know that he could have the control he wanted here in Nahar—as I said, it was obvious they were going to lose it eventually, anyway —if not to him, to someone or something else—if he'd meet their terms."

"And what were they after in exchange?"

"A guarantee that their life style and this pocket culture they'd developed would be maintained and protected."

He looked under his dark brows at me.

"I see," I said. "How did they think William could do that?"

"They didn't know. But they didn't worry about it. That's the slippery part. They just let the fact be known to William that if they got what they wanted they'd stop fighting his attempts to control Nahar directly. They left it up to him to find the ways to meet their price. That's why there's no other contract we can cite as an excuse to break this one."

I drank from my own glass.

"It sounds like William. If I know him," I said, "he'd even enjoy engineering whatever situation was needed to keep this country fifty years behind the times. But it sounded to me earlier as if you were saying that he was trying to get something out of the Dorsai at the same time. What good does it do him if you have to make a penalty payment for breaking this contract? It won't bankrupt you Graemes to pay it, will it? And even if you had to borrow from general Dorsai contingency funds, it wouldn't be more than a pinprick against those funds. Also, you still haven't explained this business of your being trapped here, not by the contract, but by the general honor of the Dorsai."

Ian nodded.

"William's taken care of both things," he said. "His plan was for the Naharese to hire Dorsai to make their army a working unit. Then his revolutionary agents would cause a revolt of that army. Then, with matters out of hand, he could step in with his own non-Dorsai officers to control the situation and bring order back to Nahar."

"I see," I said.

"He then would mediate the matter," Ian went on, "the revolutionary people would be handed some limited say in the government—under his outside control, of course—and the ranchers would give up their absolute local authority but little of anything else. They'd stay in charge of their ranches, as his managers, with all his wealth and forces to back them against any real push for control by the real revolutionary faction; which would eventually be tamed and brought in line, also—the way he's tamed and brought in line all the rest of this world, and some good-sized chunks of other worlds."

"So," I said, thoughtfully, "what he's after is to show that his military people can do things Dorsai can't?"

"You follow me," said Ian. "We command the price we do now only because military like ourselves are in limited supply. If they want Dorsai results—military

49

situations dealt with at either no cost or a minimum cost, in life and material—they have to hire Dorsai. That's as it stands now. But if it looks like others can do the same job as well or better, our price has to go down, and the Dorsai will begin to starve."

"It'd take some years for the Dorsai to starve. In that time we could live down the results of this, maybe."

"But it goes farther than that. William isn't the first to dream of being able to hire all the Dorsai and use them as a personal force to dominate the worlds. We've never considered allowing all our working people to end up in one camp. But if William can depress our price below what we need to keep the Dorsai free and independent, then he can offer us wages better than the market—survival wages, available from him alone—and we'll have no choice but to accept."

"Then you've got no choice, yourself," I said. "You've got to break this contract, no matter what it costs."

"I'm afraid not," he answered. "The cost looks right now to be the one we can't afford to pay. As I said, we're damned if we do, damned if we don't—caught in the jaws of this nutcracker unless Amanda can find us a way out—"

The door to the office where we were sitting opened at that moment and Amanda herself looked in.

"It seems some local people calling themselves the Governors have just arrived—" Her tone was humorous, but every line of her body spoke of serious concern. "Evidently, I'm supposed to go and talk with them right away. Are you coming, Ian?"

"Kensie is all you'll need," Ian said. "We've trained

them to realize that they don't necessarily get both of us on deck every time they whistle. You'll find it's just another step in the dance, anyway—there's nothing to be done with them."

"All right." She started to withdraw, stopped. "Can Padma come with us?"

"Check with Kensie. I'd say it's best not to ruffle the Governors' feathers by asking to let him sit in, right now."

"That's all right," she said. "Kensie already thought not, but he said I should ask you."

She went out.

"Sure you don't want to be there?" I asked him.

"No need." He got up. "There's something I want to show you. It's important you understand the situation here thoroughly. If Kensie and myself should both be knocked out, Amanda would only have you to help her handle things—and if you're certain about being able to stay?"

"As I said," I repeated, "I can stay."

"Fine. Come along, then. I wanted you to meet the Conde de Nahar. But I've been waiting to hear from Michael as to whether the Conde's receiving, right now. We won't wait any longer. Let's go see how the old gentleman is."

"Won't he—the Conde, I mean—be at this meeting with Amanda and the Governors?"

Ian led the way out of the room.

"Not if there's serious business to be talked about. On paper, the Conde controls everything but the Governors. They elect him. Of course, aside from the paper, they're the ones who really control everything."

We left the suite of offices and began to travel the

corridors of Gebel Nahar once more. Twice we took lift tubes and once we rode a motorized strip down one long corridor; but at the end Ian pushed open a door and we stepped into what was obviously the orderly room fronting a barracks section.

The soldier bandsman seated behind the desk there came to his feet immediately at the sight of us—or perhaps it was just at the sight of Ian.

"Sirs!" he said, in Spanish.

"I ordered Mr. de Sandoval to find out for me if the Conde would receive Captain El Man here, and myself," Ian said in the same language. "Do you know where the Bandmaster is now?"

"No, sir. He has not come back. Sir—it is not always possible to contact the Conde quickly—"

"I'm aware of that," said Ian. "Rest easy. Mr. de Sandoval's due back here shortly, then?"

"Yes, sir. Any minute now. Would the sirs care to wait in the Bandmaster's office?"

"Yes," said Ian.

The orderly turned aside, lifting his hand in a decidedly non-military gesture to usher us past his desk through a farther entrance into a larger room, very orderly and with a clean desk, but crowded with filing cabinets and with its walls hung with musical instruments.

Most of these were ones I had never seen before, although they were all variants on string or wind music-makers. There was one that looked like an early Scottish bagpipe. It had only a single drone, some seventy centimeters long, and a chanter about half that length. Another was obviously a keyed bugle of some sort, but with most of its central body length wrapped

with red cord ending in dependent tassels. I moved about the walls, examining each as I came to it, while Ian took a chair and watched me. I came back at length to the deprived bagpipe.

"Can you play this?" I asked Ian.

"I'm not a piper," said Ian. "I can blow a bit, of course—but I've never played anything but regular highland pipes. You'd better ask Michael if you want a demonstration. Apparently, he plays everything—and plays it well."

I turned away from the walls and took a seat myself.

"What do you think?" asked Ian. I was gazing around the office.

I looked back at him and saw his gaze curiously upon me.

"It's . . . strange," I said.

And the room was strange, for reasons that would probably never strike someone not a Dorsai. No two people keep an office the same way; but just as there are subtle characteristics by which one born to the Dorsai will recognize another, so there are small signals about the office of anyone on military duty and from that world. I could tell at a glance, as could Ian or any one of us, if the officer into whose room we had just stepped was Dorsai or not. The clues lie, not so much with what was in the room, as in the way the things there and the room itself was arranged. There is nothing particular to Dorsai-born individuals about such a recognition. Almost any veteran officer is able to tell you whether the owner of the office he has just stepped into is also a veteran officer, Dorsai or not. But in that case, as in this, it would be easier to give the answer than to list the reasons why the answer was what it was.

So, Michael de Sandoval's office was unmistakably the office of a Dorsai. At the same time it owned a strange difference from any other Dorsai's office, that almost shouted at us. The difference was a basic one, underneath any comparison of this place with the office of a Dorsai who had his walls hung with weapons, or with one who kept a severely clean desktop and message baskets, and preferred no weapon in sight.

"He's got these musical instruments displayed as if they were fighting tools," I said.

Ian nodded. It was not necessary to put the implication into words. If Michael had chosen to hang a banner from one of the walls testifying to the fact that he would absolutely refuse to lay his hands upon a weapon, he could not have announced himself more plainly to Ian and myself.

"It seems to be a strong point with him," I said. "I wonder what happened?"

"His business, of course," said Ian.

"Yes," I said.

But the discovery hurt me—because suddenly I identified what I had felt in young Michael from the first moment I had met him, here on Ceta. It was pain, a deep and abiding pain; and you cannot have known someone since he was in childhood and not be moved by that sort of pain.

The orderly stuck his head into the room.

"Sirs," he said, "the Bandmaster comes. He'll be here in one minute."

"Thank you," said Ian.

A moment later, Michael came in.

"Sorry to keep you waiting—" he began.

"Perfectly all right," Ian said. "The Conde made

you wait yourself before letting you speak with him, didn't he?"

"Yes sir."

"Well, is he available now, to be met by me and Captain El Man?"

"Yes sir. You're both most welcome."

"Good."

Ian stood up and so did I. We went out, followed by Michael to the door of his office.

"Amanda Morgan is seeing the Governors, at the moment," Ian said to him as we left him. "She may want to talk to you after that's over. You might keep yourself available for her."

"I'll be right here," said Michael. "Sir—I wanted to apologize for my orderly's making excuses about my not being here when you came—" he glanced over at the orderly who was looking embarrassed. "My men have been told not to—"

"It's all right, Michael," said Ian. "You'd be an unusual Dorsai if they didn't try to protect you."

"Still—" said Michael.

"Still," said Ian. "I know they've trained only as bandmen. They may be line troops at the moment—all the line troops we've got to hold this place with—but I'm not expecting miracles."

"Well," said Michael. "Thank you, Commander."

"You're welcome."

We went out. Once more Ian led me through a maze of corridors and lifts.

"How many of his band decided to stay with him when the regiments moved out?" I asked as we went.

"All of them," said Ian.

"And no one else stayed?"

Ian looked at me with a glint of humor.

"You have to remember," he said, "Michael did graduate from the Academy, after all."

A final short distance down a wide corridor brought us to a massive pair of double doors. Ian touched a visitor's button on the right-hand door and spoke to an annunciator panel in Spanish.

"Commander Ian Graeme and Captain El Man are here with permission to see the Conde."

There was the pause of a moment and then one of the doors opened to show us another of Michael's bandsmen.

"Be pleased to come in, sirs," he said.

"Thank you," Ian said as we walked past. "Where's the Conde's majordomo?"

"He is gone, sir. Also most of the other servants."

"I see."

The room we had just been let into was a wide lobby filled with enormous and magnificently-kept furniture but lacking any windows. The bandman led us through two more rooms like it, also without windows, until we were finally ushered into a third and finally window-walled room, with the same unchanging view of the plains below. A stick-thin old man dressed in black was standing with the help of a silver-headed cane, before the center of the window area.

The soldier faded out of the room. Ian led me to the old man.

"El Conde," he said, still in Spanish, "may I introduce Captain Corunna El Man. Captain, you have the honor of meeting El Conde de Nahar, Macias Francisco Ramón Manuel Valentin y Compostela y Abente."

"You are welcome, Captain El Man," said the Con-

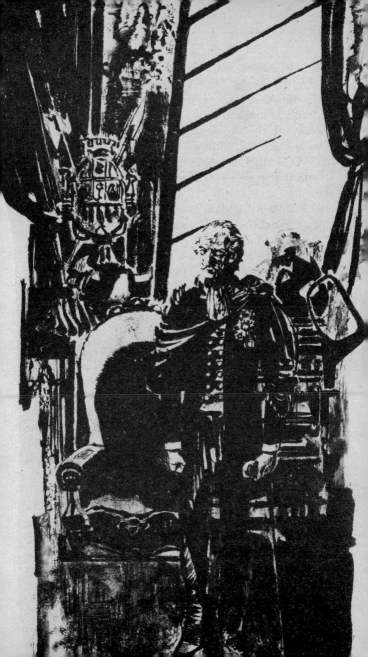

de. He spoke a more correct, if more archaic, Spanish than that of the other Naharese I had so far met; and his voice was the thin remnant of what once must have been a remarkable bass. "We will sit down now, if you please. If my age produces a weakness, it is that it is wearisome to stand for any length of time."

We settled ourselves in heavy, overstuffed chairs with massively padded arms—more like thrones than chairs.

"Captain El Man," said Ian, "happened to be on leave, back on the Dorsai. He volunteered to bring Amanda Morgan here to discuss the present situation with the Governors. She's talking to them now."

"I have not met. . ." the Conde hesitated over her name, "Amanda Morgan."

"She is one of our experts of the sort that the present situation calls for."

"I would like to meet her."

"She's looking forward to meeting you."

"Possibly this evening? I would have liked to have had all of you to dinner, but you know, I suppose, that most of my servants have gone."

"I just learned that," said Ian.

"They may go," said the Conde. "They will not be allowed to return. Nor will the regiments who have deserted their duty be allowed to return to my armed forces."

"With the Conde's indulgence," said Ian, "we don't yet know all the reasons for their leaving. It may be that some leniency is justified."

"I can think of none." The Conde's voice was thin with age, but his back was as erect as a flagstaff and his dark eyes did not waver. "But, if you think there is some reason for it, I can reserve judgment momentarily."

"We'd appreciate that," Ian said.

"You are very lenient." The Conde looked at me. His voice took on an unexpected timbre. "Captain, has the Commander here told you? Those deserters out there—" he flicked a finger toward the window and the plains beyond, "under the instigation of people calling themselves revolutionaries, have threatened to take over Gebel Nahar. If they dare to come here, I and what few loyal servants remain will resist. To the death!"

"The Governors—" Ian began.

"The Governors have nothing to say in the matter!" the Conde turned fiercely on him. "Once, they—their fathers and grandfathers, rather—chose my father to be El Conde. I inherited that title and neither they, nor anyone else in the universe has the authority to take it from me. While I live, I will be El Conde; and the only way I will cease to be El Conde will be when death takes me. I will remain, I will fight—alone if need be —as long as I am able. But I will retreat, never! I will compromise, *never!*"

He continued to talk, for some minutes; but although his words changed, the message of them remained the same. He would not give an inch to anyone who wished to change the governmental system in Nahar. If he had been obviously uninformed or ignorant of the implications of what he was saying, it would have been easy to let his words blow by unheeded. But this was obviously not the case. His frailty was all in the thin old body. His mind was not only clear but fully aware of the situation. What he announced was simply an unshakable determination never to yield in spite of reason or the overwhelming odds against him.

After a while he ran down. He apologized graciously for his emotion, but not for his attitude; and, after a few minutes more of meaninglessly polite conversation on the history of Gebel Nahar itself, let us leave.

"So you see part of our problem," said Ian to me when we were alone again, walking back to his offices.

We went a little distance together in silence.

"Part of that problem," I said, "seems to lie in the difference between our idea of honor, and theirs, here."

"And William's complete lack of it," said Ian. "You're right. With us, honor's a matter of the individual's obligation to himself and his community —which can end up being to the human race in general. To the Naharese, honor's an obligation only to their own soul."

I laughed, involuntarily.

"I'm sorry," I said, as he looked at me. "But you hit it almost too closely. Did you ever read Calderon's poem about the Mayor of Zalamea?"

"I don't think so. Calderon?"

"Pedro Calderon de la Barca, seventeenth century Spanish poet. He wrote a poem called *El Alcalde de Zalamea.*"

I gave him the lines he had reminded me of.

> *Al Rey la hacienda y la vida*
> *Se ha de dar; pero el honor*
> *Es patrimonio del alma*
> *Y el alma soló es de Dios.*

" '—*Fortune and life we owe to the King,*' " murmured

Ian, " *'but honor is patrimony of the soul and the soul belongs to God alone.'* I see what you mean."

I started to say something, then decided it was too much effort. I was aware of Ian glancing sideways at me as we went.

"When did you eat last?" he asked.

"I don't remember," I said. "But I don't particularly need food right now."

"You need sleep, then," said Ian, "I'm not surprised, after the way you made it here from the Dorsai. When we get back to the office, I'll call one of Michael's men to show you your quarters, and you'd better sleep in. I can make your excuses to the Conde if he still wants us all to get together tonight."

"Yes. Good," I said. "I'd appreciate that."

Now that I had admitted to tiredness, it was an effort even to think. For those who have never navigated between the stars, it is easy to forget the implications in the fact that the danger increases rapidly with the distance moved in a single shift—beyond a certain safe amount of light-years. We had exceeded safe limits as far as I had dared push them on each of the six shifts that had brought Amanda and myself to Ceta.

It's not just that danger—the danger of finding yourself with so large an error in destination that you cannot recognize any familiar star patterns from which to navigate. It is the fact that even when you emerge in known space, a large error factor requires infinitely more recalculation to locate your position. It is vital to locate yourself to a fine enough point so that your error on the next shift will not be compounded and you will find yourself lost beyond repair.

For three days I had had no more than catnaps be-

tween periods of calculation. I was numb with a fatigue I had held at bay until this moment with the body adrenalin that can be evoked to meet an emergency situation.

When the bandsman supplied by Ian had shown me at last to a suite of rooms, I found I wanted nothing more than to collapse on the enormous bed in the bedroom. But years of instinct made me prowl the quarters first and check them out. My suite consisted of three rooms and bathroom; and it had the inevitable plains-facing window wall—with one difference. This one had a door in it to let me out onto a small balcony that ran the length of this particular level. It was divided into a semi-private outdoor area for each suite by tall plants in pots which acted as screens at each division point.

I checked the balcony area and the suite, locked the doors to the hall and to the balcony, and slept.

It was sometime after dark when I awoke, suddenly. I was awake and sitting up on the edge of the bed in one reflex movement before it registered that what had roused me had been the sound of the call chime at the front door of my suite.

I reached over and keyed on the annunciator circuit. "Yes?" I said. "Who is it?"

"Michael de Sandoval," said Michael's voice, "can I come in?"

I touched the stud that unlocked the door. It swung open, letting a knife-blade sharp swath of light from the corridor into the darkness of my sitting room, as seen through the entrance from my bedroom. I was up on my feet now, and moving to meet him in the sitting room. He entered and the door closed behind him.

"What is it?" I asked.

"The ventilating system is out on this level," he said; and I realized that the air in the suite was now perfectly motionless—motionless and beginning to be a little warm and stuffy. Evidently Gebel Nahar had been designed to be sealed against outside atmosphere.

"I wanted to check the quarters of everyone on this level," Michael said. "Interior doors aren't so tight that you would have asphyxiated; but the breathing could have got a little heavy. Maybe by morning we can locate what's out of order and fix it. This is part of the problem of the servant staff taking off when the army did. I'd suggest that I open the door to the balcony for you, sir."

He was already moving across the room toward the door he had mentioned.

"Thanks," I said. "What was the situation with the servants? Were they revolutionary sympathizers, too?"

"Not necessarily." He unlocked the door and propped it open to the night air, which came coolly and sweetly through the aperture. "They just didn't want their throats cut along with the Conde's, when the army stormed its way back in here."

"I see," I said.

"Yes." He came back to me in the center of the sitting room.

"What time is it?" I asked. "I've been sleeping as if I was under drugs."

"A little before midnight."

I sat down in one of the chairs of the unlighted lounge. The glow of the soft exterior lights spaced at ten meter intervals along the outer edge of the balcony came through the window wall and dimly illuminated the room.

"Sit for a moment," I said. "Tell me. How did the meeting with the Conde go this evening?"

He took a chair facing me.

"I should be getting back soon," he said. "I'm the only one we've got available for a duty officer at the moment. But—the meeting with the Conde went like a charm. He was so busy being gracious to Amanda he almost forgot to breathe defiance against the army deserters."

"How did Amanda do with the Governors, do you know?"

I sensed, rather than saw, a shrug of his shoulders in the gloom.

"There was nothing much to be done with them," he said. "They talked about their concern over the desertion of the regiments and wanted reassurances that Ian and Kensie could handle the situation. Effectively, it was all choreographed."

"They've left, then?"

"That's right. They asked for guarantees for the safety of the Conde. Both Ian and Kensie told them that there was no such thing as a guarantee; but we'd protect the Conde, of course, with every means at our disposal. Then they left."

"It sounds," I said, "as if Amanda could have saved her time and effort."

"No. She said she wanted to get the feel of them." He leaned forward. "You know, she's something to write home about. I think if anyone can find a way out of this, she can. She says herself that there's no question that there is a way out—it's just that finding it in the next twenty-four to thirty-six hours is asking a lot."

"Has she checked with you about these people? You seem to be the only one around who knows them at all well."

"She talked with me when we flew in—you remember. I told her I'd be available any time she needed me. So far, however, she's spent most of her time either working by herself, or with Ian or Padma."

"I see," I said. "Is there anything I can do? Would you like me to spell you on the duty officer bit?"

"You're to rest, Ian says. He'll need you tomorrow. I'm getting along fine with my duties." He moved toward the front door of the suite. "Good night."

"Good night," I said.

He went out, the knife of light from the corridor briefly cutting across the carpeting of my sitting room and vanishing again as the door opened, then latched behind him.

I stayed where I was in the sitting room chair, enjoying the gentle night breeze through the propped-open door. I may have dozed. At any rate I came to, suddenly, to the sound of voices from the balcony. Not from my portion of the balcony, but from the portion next to it, beyond my bedroom window to the left.

". . . yes," a voice was saying. Ian had been in my mind; and for a second I thought I was hearing Ian speak. But it was Kensie. The voices were identical; only, there was a difference in attitude that distinguished them.

"I don't know. . ." it was Amanda's voice answering, a troubled voice.

"Time goes by quickly," Kensie said. "Look at us. It was just yesterday we were in school together."

"I know," she said, "you're talking about it being time to settle down. But maybe I never will."

"How sure are you of that?"

"Not sure, of course." Her voice changed as if she had moved some little distance from him. I had an unexpected mental image of him standing back by the door in a window wall through which they had just come out together; and one of her, having just turned and walked to the balcony railing, where she now stood with her back to him, looking out at the night and the starlit plain.

"Then you could take the idea of settling down under consideration."

"No," she said. "I know I don't want to do that."

Her voice changed again, as if she had turned and come back to him. "Maybe I'm ghost-ridden, Kensie. Maybe it's the old spirit of the first Amanda that's ruling out the ordinary things for me."

"She married—three times."

"But her husbands weren't important to her, that way. Oh, I know she loved them. I've read her letters and what her children wrote down about her after they were adults themselves. But she really belonged to everyone, not just to her husbands and children. Don't you understand? I think that's the way it's going to have to be for me, too."

He said nothing. After a long moment she spoke again, and her voice was lowered, and drastically altered.

"Kensie! Is it that important?"

His voice was lightly humorous, but the words came a fraction more slowly than they had before.

"It seems to be."

"But it's something we both just fell into, as children. It was just an assumption on both our parts. Since then, we've grown up. You've changed. I've changed."

"Yes."

"You don't need me. Kensie, you don't need *me*—" her voice was soft. "Everybody loves you."

"Could I trade?" The humorous tone persisted. "Everybody for you?"

"Kensie, don't!"

"You ask a lot," he said; and now the humor was gone, but there was still nothing in the way he spoke that reproached her. "I'd probably find it easier to stop breathing."

There was another silence.

"Why can't you see? I don't have any other choice," she said. "I don't have any more choice than you do. We're both what we are, and stuck with what we are."

"Yes," he said.

The silence this time lasted a long time. But they did not move, either of them. By this time my ear was sensitized to sounds as light as the breathing of a sparrow. They had been standing a little apart, and they stayed standing apart.

"Yes," he said again, finally—and this time it was a long, slow *yes*, a tired *yes*. "Life moves. And all of us move with it, whether we like it or not."

She moved to him, now. I heard her steps on the concrete floor of the balcony.

"You're exhausted," she said. "You and Ian both. Get some rest before tomorrow. Things'll look different in the daylight."

"That sometimes happens." The touch of humor was back, but there was effort behind it. "Not that I believe it for a moment, in this case."

They went back inside.

I sat where I was, wide awake. There had been no way for me to get up and get away from their conversation without letting them know I was there. Their hearing was at least as good as mine, and like me they had been trained to keep their senses always alert. But knowing all that did not help. I still had the ugly feeling that I had been intruding where I should not have been.

There was no point in moving now. I sat where I was, trying to talk sense to myself and get the ugly

feeling under control. I was so concerned with my own
feelings that for once I did not pay close attention to
the sounds around me, and the first warning I had was
a small noise in my own entrance to the balcony area;
and I looked up to see the dark silhouette of a woman
in the doorway.

"You heard," Amanda's voice said.

There was no point in denying it.

"Yes," I told her.

She stayed where she was, standing in the doorway.

"I happened to be sitting here when you came out
on the balcony," I said. "There was no chance to shut
the door or move away."

"It's all right," she came in. "No, don't turn on the light."

I dropped the hand I had lifted toward the control studs in the arm of my chair. With the illumination from the balcony behind her, she could see me better than I could see her. She sat down in the chair Michael had occupied a short while before.

"I told myself I'd step over and see if you were sleeping all right," she said. "Ian has a lot of work in mind for you tomorrow. But I think I was really hoping to find you awake."

Even through the darkness, the signals came loud and clear. My geas was at work again.

"I don't want to intrude," I said.

"If I reach out and haul you in by the scruff of the neck, are you intruding?" Her voice had the same sort of lightness overlying pain that I had heard in Kensie's. "I'm the one who's thinking of intruding—of intruding my problems on you."

"That's not necessarily an intrusion," I said.

"I hoped you'd feel that way," she said. It was strange to have her voice coming in such everyday tones from a silhouette of darkness. "I wouldn't bother you, but I need to have all my mind on what I'm doing here and personal matters have ended up getting in the way."

She paused.

"You don't really mind people spilling all over you, do you?" she said.

"No," I said.

"I thought so. I got the feeling you wouldn't. Do you think of Else much?"

"When other things aren't on my mind."

"I wish I'd known her."

"She was someone to know."

"Yes. Knowing someone else is what makes the difference. The trouble is, often we don't know. Or we don't know until too late." She paused. "I suppose you think, after what you heard just now, that I'm talking about Kensie?"

"Aren't you?"

"No. Kensie and Ian—the Graemes are so close to us Morgans that we might as well all be related. You don't usually fall in love with a relative—or you don't think you will, at least, when you're young. The kind of person you imagine falling in love with is someone strange and exciting—someone from fifty light years away."

"I don't know about that," I said. "Else was a neighbor and I think I grew up being in love with her."

"I'm sorry." Her silhouette shifted a little in the darkness. "I'm really just talking about myself. But I know what you mean. In sober moments, when I was younger, I more or less just assumed that some day I'd wind up with Kensie. You'd have to have something wrong with you not to want someone like him."

"And you've got something wrong with you?" I said.

"Yes," she said. "That's it. I grew up, that's the trouble."

"Everybody does."

"I don't mean I grew up, physically. I mean, I matured. We live a long time, we Morgans, and I suppose we're slower growing up than most. But you know how it is with young anythings—young animals as well as young humans. Did you ever have a wild animal as a pet as a child?"

"Several," I said.

"Then you've run into what I'm talking about. While the wild animal's young, it's cuddly and tame; but when it grows up, the day comes it bites or slashes at you without warning. People talk about that being part of their wild nature. But it isn't. Humans change just exactly the same way. When anything young grows up, it becomes conscious of itself, its own wants, its own desires, its own moods. Then the day comes when someone tries to play with it and it isn't in a playing mood—and it reacts with *'Back off! What I want is just as important as what you want!'* And all at once, the time of its being young and cuddly is over forever."

"Of course," I said. "That happens to all of us."

"But to us—to our people—it happens too late!" she said. "Or rather, we start life too early. By the age of seventeen on the Dorsai we have to be out and working like an adult, either at home or on some other world. We're pitchforked into adulthood. There's never any time to take stock, to realize what being adult is going to turn us into. We don't realize we aren't cubs any more until one day we slash or bite someone without warning; and then we realize that we've changed —and they've changed. But it's too late for us to adjust to the change in the other person because we've already been trapped by our own change."

She stopped. I sat, not speaking, waiting. From my experience with this sort of thing since Else died, I assumed that I no longer needed to talk. She would carry the conversation, now.

"No, it wasn't Kensie I was talking about when I first came in here and I said the trouble is you don't know someone else until too late. It's Ian."

"Ian?" I said, for she had stopped again, and now I felt with equal instinct that she needed some help to continue.

"Yes," she said. "When I was young, I didn't understand Ian. I do now. Then, I thought there was nothing to him—or else he was simply solid all the way through, like a piece of wood. But he's not. Everything you can see in Kensie is there in Ian, only there's no light to see it by. Now I know. And now it's too late."

"Too late?" I said. "He's not married, is he?"

"Married? Not yet. But you didn't know? Look at

the picture on his desk. Her name's Leah. She's on
Earth. He met her when he was there, four years ago.
But that's not what I mean by too late. I mean—it's
too late for me. What you heard me tell Kensie is the
truth. I've got the curse of the first Amanda. I'm born
to belong to a lot of people, first; and only to any single
person, second. As much as I'd give for Ian, that
equation's there in me, ever since I grew up. Sooner or
later it'd put even him in second place for me. I can't
do that to him; and it's too late for me to be anything
else."

"Maybe Ian'd be willing to agree to those terms."

She did not answer for a second. Then I heard a
slow intake of breath from the darker darkness that
was her.

"You shouldn't say that," she said.

There was a second of silence. Then she spoke
again, fiercely.

"Would you suggest something like that to Ian if our
positions were reversed?"

"I didn't suggest it," I said. "I mentioned it."

Another pause.

"You're right," she said. "I know what I want and
what I'm afraid of in myself, and it seems to me so
obvious I keep thinking everyone else must know too."

She stood up.

"Forgive me, Corunna," she said. "I've got no right
to burden you with all this."

"It's the way the world is," I said. "People talk to
people."

"And to you, more than most." She went toward the
door to the balcony and paused in it. "Thanks again."

"I've done nothing," I said.

"Thank you anyway. Good night. Sleep if you can."

She stepped out through the door; and through the window wall I watched her, very erect, pass to my left until she walked out of my sight beyond the sitting room wall.

I went back to bed, not really expecting to fall asleep again easily. But I dropped off and slept like a log.

When I woke it was morning, and my bedside phone was chiming. I flicked it on and Michael looked at me out of the screen.

"I'm sending a man up with maps of the interior of Gebel Nahar," he said, "so you can find your way around. Breakfast's available in the General Staff Lounge, if you're ready."

"Thanks," I told him.

I got up and was ready when the bandsman he had sent arrived, with a small display cube holding the maps. I took it with me and the bandsman showed me to the General Staff Lounge—which, it turned out, was not a lounge for the staff of Gebel Nahar, in general, but one for the military commanders of that establishment. Ian was the only other present when I got there and he was just finishing his meal.

"Sit down," he said.

I sat.

"I'm going ahead on the assumption that I'll be defending this place in twenty-four hours or so," he said. "What I'd like you to do is familiarize yourself with its defenses, particularly the first line of walls and its weapons, so that you can either direct the men working them, or take over the general defense, if necessary."

"What have you got in mind for a general defense?"

I asked, as a bandsman came out of the kitchen area to see what I would eat. I told him and he went.

"We've got just about enough of Michael's troops to man that first wall and have a handful in reserve," he said. "Most of them have never touched anything but a handweapon in their life, but we've got to use them to fight with the emplaced energy weapons against foot attack up the slope. I'd like you to get them on the weapons and drill them—Michael should be able to help you, since he knows which of them are steady and which aren't. Get breakfast in you; and I'll tell you what I expect the regiments to do on the attack and what I think we might do when they try it."

He went on talking while my food came and I ate. Boiled down, his expectations—based on what he had learned of the Naharese military while he had been here, and from consultation with Michael—were for a series of infantry wave attacks up the slope until the first wall was overrun. His plan called for a defense of the first wall until the last safe moment, destruction of the emplaced weapons, so they could not be turned against us, and a quick retreat to the second wall with its weapons—and so, step by step retreating up the terraces. It was essentially the sort of defense that Gebel Nahar had been designed for by its builders.

The problem would be getting absolutely green and excitable troops like the Naharese bandsmen to retreat cool-headedly on order. If they could not be brought to do that, and lingered behind, then the first wave over the ramparts could reduce their numbers to the point where there would not be enough of them to make any worthwhile defense of the second terrace, to say nothing of the third, the fourth, and so on, and still

have men left for a final stand within the fortress-like walls of the top three levels.

Given an equal number of veteran, properly trained troops, to say nothing of Dorsai-trained ones, we might even have held Gebel Nahar in that fashion and inflicted enough casualties on the attackers to eventually make them pull back. But unspoken between Ian and myself as we sat in the lounge, was the fact that the most we could hope to do with what we had was inflict a maximum of damage while losing.

However, again unspoken between us, was the fact that the stiffer our defense of Gebel Nahar, even in a hopeless situation, the more difficult it would be for the Governors and William to charge the Dorsai officers with incompetence of defense.

I finished eating and got up to go.

"Where's Amanda?" I asked.

"She's working with Padma—or maybe I should put it that Padma's working with her," Ian said.

"I didn't know Exotics took sides."

"He isn't," Ian said. "He's just making knowledge —his knowledge—available to someone who needs it. That's standard Exotic practice as you know as well as I do. He and Amanda are still hunting some political angle to bring us and the Dorsai out of this without prejudice."

"What do you really think their chances are?"

Ian shook his head.

"But," he said, shuffling together the papers he had spread out before him on the lounge table, "of course, where they're looking is away out, beyond the areas of strategy I know. We can hope."

"Did you ever stop to think that possibly Michael,

with his knowledge of these Naharese, could give them some insights they wouldn't otherwise have?" I asked.

"Yes," he said. "I told them both that; and told Michael to make himself available to them if they thought they could use him. So far, I don't think they have."

He got up, holding his papers and we went out; I to the band quarters and Michael's office, he to his own office and the overall job of organizing our supplies and everything else necessary for the defense.

Michael was not in his office. The orderly directed me to the first wall, where I found him already drilling his men on the emplaced weapons there. I worked with him for most of the morning; and then we stopped, not because there was not a lot more practice needed, but because his untrained troops were exhausted and beginning to make mistakes simply out of fatigue.

Michael sent them to lunch. He and I went back to his office and had sandwiches and coffee brought in by his orderly.

"What about this?" I asked, after we were done, getting up and going to the wall where the archaic-looking bagpipe hung. "I asked Ian about it. But he said he'd only played highland pipes and that if I wanted a demonstration, I should ask you."

Michael looked up from his seat behind his desk, and grinned. The drill on the guns seemed to have done something for him in a way he was not really aware of himself. He looked younger and more cheerful than I had yet seen him; and obviously he enjoyed any attention given to his instruments.

"That's a *gaita gallega*," he said. "Or, to be correct, it's a local imitation of the gaita gallega you can still find occasionally being made and played in the province of Galicia in Spain, back on Earth. It's a perfectly playable instrument to anyone who's familiar with the highland pipes. Ian could have played it—I'd guess he just thought I might prefer to show it off myself."

"He seemed to think you could play it better," I said.

"Well. . ." Michael grinned again. "Perhaps, a bit."

He got up and came over to the wall with me.

"Do you really want to hear it?" he asked.

"Yes, I do."

He took it down from the wall.

"We'll have to step outside," he said. "It's not the sort of instrument to be played in a small room like this."

We went back out on to the first terrace by the deserted weapon emplacements. He swung the pipe up in his arms, the long single drone with its fringe tied at the two ends of the drone, resting on his left shoulder and pointing up into the air behind him. He took the mouthpiece between his lips and laid his fingers across the holes of the chanter. Then he blew up the bag and began to play.

The music of the pipes is like Dorsai whiskey. People either cannot stand it, or they feel that there's nothing comparable. I happen to be one of those who love the sound—for no good reason, I would have said until that trip to Gebel Nahar; since my own heritage is Spanish rather than Scottish and I had never before realized that it was also a Spanish instrument.

Michael played something Scottish and standard—*The Flowers of the Forest,* I think—pacing slowly up and down as he played. Then, abruptly he swung around

and stepped out, almost strutted, in fact; and played something entirely different.

I wish there were words in me to describe it. It was anything but Scottish. It was hispanic, right down to its backbones—a wild, barbaric, musically ornate challenge of some sort that heated the blood in my veins and threatened to raise the hair on the back of my neck.

He finished at last with a sort of dying wail as he swung the deflating bag down from his shoulder. His face was not young any more, it was changed. He looked drawn and old.

"What was that?" I demanded.

"It's got a polite name for polite company," he said. "But nobody uses it. The Naharese call it *Su Madre*."

"*Your Mother?*" I echoed. Then, of course, it hit me. The Spanish language has a number of elaborate and poetically insulting curses to throw at your enemy about his ancestry; and the words *su madre* are found in most of them.

"Yes," said Michael. "It's what you play when you're daring the enemy to come out and fight. It accuses him of being less than a man in all the senses of that phrase—and the Naharese love it."

He sat down on the rampart of the terrace, suddenly, like someone very tired and discouraged by a long and hopeless effort, resting the gaita gallega on his knees.

"And they like me," he said, staring blindly at the wall of the barrack area, behind me. "My bandsmen, my regiment—they like me."

"There're always exceptions," I said, watching him. "But usually the men who serve under them like their Dorsai officers."

"That's not what I mean." He was still staring at the wall. "I've made no secret here of the fact I won't touch a weapon. They all knew it from the day I signed on as bandmaster."

"I see," I said. "So that's it."

He looked up at me, abruptly.

"Do you know how they react to cowards—as they consider them—people who are able to fight but won't, in this particular crazy splinter culture? They encourage them to get off the face of the earth. They show their manhood by knocking cowards around here. But they don't touch me. They don't even challenge me to duels."

"Because they don't believe you," I said.

"That's it." His face was almost savage. "They don't. Why won't they believe me?"

"Because you only *say* you won't use a weapon," I told him bluntly. "In every other language you speak, everything you say or do, you broadcast just the opposite information. That tells them that not only can you use a weapon, but that you're so good at it none of them who'd challenge you would stand a chance. You could not only defeat someone like that, you could make him look foolish in the process. And no one wants to look foolish, particularly a macho-minded individual. That message is in the very way you walk and talk. How else could it be, with you?"

"That's not true!" he got suddenly to his feet, holding the gaita. "I live what I believe in. I have, ever since—"

He stopped.

"Maybe we'd better get back to work," I said, as gently as I could.

"No!" The word burst out of him. "I want to tell someone. The oods are we're not going to be around after this. I want someone to. . ."

He broke off. He had been about to say "someone to understand. . ." and he had not been able to get the words out. But I could not help him. As I've said, since Else's death, I've grown accustomed to listening to people. But there is something in me that tells me when to speak and when not to help them with what they wish to say. And now I was being held silent.

He struggled with himself for a few seconds, and then calm seemed to flow over him.

"No," he said, as if talking to himself, "what people think doesn't matter. We're not likely to live through this, and I want to know how you react."

He looked at me.

"That's why I've got to explain it to someone like you," he said. "I've got to know how they'd take it, back home, if I'd explained it to them. And your family is the same as mine, from the same canton, the same neighborhood, the same sort of ancestry. . ."

"Did it occur to you you might not owe anyone an explanation?" I said. "When your parents raised you, they only paid back the debt they owed their parents for raising them. If you've got any obligation to anyone —and even that's a moot point, since the idea behind our world is that it's a planet of free people—it's to the Dorsai in general, to bring in interstellar exchange credits by finding work off-planet. And you've done that by becoming bandmaster here. Anything beyond that's your own private business."

It was quite true. The vital currency between worlds was not wealth, as every schoolchild knows, but the exchange of interplanetary work credits. The inhabited worlds trade special skills and knowledges, packaged in human individuals; and the exchange credits earned by a Dorsai on Newton enables the Dorsai to hire a geophysicist from Newton—or a physician from Kultis. In addition to his personal pay, Michael had been earning exchange credits ever since he had come here. True, he might have earned these at a higher rate if he had chosen work as a mercenary combat officer; but the exchange credits he did earn as bandmaster more than justified the expense of his education and training.

"I'm not talking about that—" he began.

"No," I said, "you're talking about a point of obligation and honor not very much removed from the sort of thing these Naharese have tied themselves up with."

He stood for a second, absorbing that. But his mouth was tight and his jaw set.

"What you're telling me," he said at last, "is that you don't want to listen. I'm not surprised."

"Now," I said, "you really are talking like a Naharese. I'll listen to anything you want to say, of course."

"Then sit down," he said.

He gestured to the rampart and sat down himself. I came and perched there, opposite him.

"Do you know I'm a happy man?" he demanded. "I really am. Why not? I've got everything I want. I've got a military job, I'm in touch with all the things that I grew up feeling made the kind of life one of my family ought to have. I'm one of a kind. I'm better at what I do and everything connected with it than anyone else

they can find—and I've got my other love, which was music, as my main duty. My men like me, my regiment is proud of me. My superiors like me."

I nodded.

"But then there's this other part. . ." His hands closed on the bag of the gaita, and there was a faint sound from the drone.

"Your refusal to fight?"

"Yes." He got up from the ramparts and began to pace back and forth, holding the instrument, talking a little jerkily. "This feeling against hurting anything . . . I had it, too, just as long as I had the other—all the dreams I made up as a boy from the stories the older people in the family told me. When I was young it didn't seem to matter to me that the feeling and the dreams hit head on. It just always happened that, in my own personal visions the battles I won were always bloodless, the victories always came with no one getting hurt. I didn't worry about any conflict in me, then. I thought it was something that would take care of itself later, as I grew up. You don't kill anyone when you're going through the Academy, of course. You know as well as I do that the better you are, the less of a danger you are to your fellow-students. But what was in me didn't change. It was there with me all the time, not changing."

"No normal person likes the actual fighting and killing," I said. "What sets us Dorsai off in a class by ourselves is the fact that most of the time we *can* win bloodlessly, where someone else would have dead bodies piled all over the place. Our way justifies itself to our employers by saving them money; but it also gets us away from the essential brutality of combat and

keeps us human. No good officer pins medals on himself in proportion to the people he kills and wounds.
Remember what Cletus says about that? He hated
what you hate, just as much."

"But he could do it when he had to," Michael
stopped and looked at me with a face, the skin of which
was drawn tight over the bones. "So can you, now. Or
Ian. Or Kensie."

That was true, of course. I could not deny it.

"You see," said Michael, "that's the difference between out on the worlds and back at the Academy. In life, sooner or later, you get to the killing part. Sooner or later, if you live by the sword, you kill with the sword. When I graduated and had to face going out to the worlds as a fighting officer, I finally had to make that decision. And so I did. I can't hurt anyone. I won't hurt anyone—even to save my own life, I think. But at the same time I'm a soldier and nothing else. I'm bred and born a soldier. I don't want any other life, I can't conceive of any other life; and I love it."

He broke off, abruptly. For a long moment he stood, staring out over the plains at the distant flashes of light from the camp of the deserted regiments.

"Well, there it is," he said.

"Yes," I said.

He turned to look at me.

"Will you tell my family that?" he asked. "If you should get home and I don't?"

"If it comes to that, I will," I said. "But we're a long way from being dead, yet."

He grinned, unexpectedly, a sad grin.

"I know," he said. "It's just that I've had this on my conscience for a long time. You don't mind?"

"Of course not."

"Thanks," he said.

He hefted the gaita in his hands as if he had just suddenly remembered that he held it.

"My men will be back out here in about fifteen minutes," he said. "I can carry on with the drilling myself, if you've got other things you want to do."

I looked at him a little narrowly.

"What you're trying to tell me," I said, "is that they'll learn faster if I'm not around."

"Something like that." He laughed. "They're used to me; but you make them self-conscious. They tighten up and keep making the same mistakes over and over again; and then they get into a fury with themselves and do even worse. I don't know if Ian would approve, but I do know these people; and I think I can bring them along faster alone. . ."

"Whatever works," I said. "I'll go and see what else Ian can find for me to do."

I turned and went to the door that would let me back into the interior of Gebel Nahar.

"Thank you again," he called after me. There was a note of relief in his voice that moved me more strongly than I had expected, so that instead of telling him that what I had done in listening to him was nothing at all, I simply waved at him and went inside.

I found my way back to Ian's office, but he was not there. It occurred to me, suddenly, that Kensie, Padma or Amanda might know where he had gone—and they should all be at work in other offices of that same suite.

I went looking, and found Kensie with his desk covered with large scale printouts of terrain maps.

"Ian?" he said. "No, I don't know. But he ought to be back in his office soon. I'll have some work for you tonight, by the way. I want to mine the approach slope. Michael's bandsmen can do the actual work, after they've had some rest from the day; but you and I are going to need to go out first and make a sweep to pick up any observers they've sent from the regiments to camp outside our walls. Then, later, before dawn

LOST DORSAI

I'd like some of us to do a scout of that camp of theirs on the plains and get some hard ideas as to how many of them there are, what they have to attack with, and so on. . ."

"Fine," I said. "I'm all slept up now, myself. Call on me when you want me."

"You could try asking Amanda or Padma if they know where Ian is."

"I was just going to."

Amanda and Padma were in a conference room two doors down from Kensie's office, seated at one end of a long table covered with text printouts and with an activated display screen flat in its top. Amanda was studying the screen and they both looked up as I put my head in the door. But while Padma's eyes were sharp and questioning, Amanda's were abstract, like the eyes of someone refusing to be drawn all the way back from whatever was engrossing her.

"Just a question. . ." I said.

"I'll come," Padma said to me. He turned to Amanda. "You go on."

She went back to her contemplation of the screen without a word. Padma got up and came to me, stepping into the outside room and shutting the door behind him.

"I'm trying to find Ian."

"I don't know where he'd be just now," said Padma. "Around Gebel Nahar somewhere—but saying that's not much help."

"Not at the size of this establishment," I nodded toward the door he had just shut.

"It's getting rather late, isn't it," I asked, "for Amanda to hope to turn up some sort of legal solution?"

"Not necessarily." The outer office we were standing in had its own window wall, and next to that window wall were several of the heavily overstuffed armchairs that were a common article of furniture in the place. "Why don't we sit down there? If he comes in from the corridor, he's got to go through this office, and if he comes out on the terrace of this level, we can see him through the window."

We went over and took chairs.

"It's not exact, actually, to say that there's a legal way of handling this situation that Amanda's looking for. I thought you understood that?"

"Her work is something I don't know a thing about," I told him. "It's a specialty that grew up as we got more and more aware that the people we were making contracts with might have different meanings for the same words, and different notions of implied obligations, than we had. So we've developed people like Amanda, who steep themselves in the differences of attitude and idea we might run into, in the splinter cultures we deal with."

"I know," he said.

"Yes, of course you would, wouldn't you?"

"Not inevitably," he said. "It happens that as an Outbond, I wrestle with pretty much the same sort of problems that Amanda does. My work is with people who aren't Exotics, and my responsibility most of the time is to make sure we understand them—and they us. That's why I say what we have here goes far beyond legal matters."

"For example?" I found myself suddenly curious.

"You might get a better word picture if you said what Amanda is searching for is a *social* solution to the situation."

"I see," I said. "This morning Ian talked about Amanda saying that there always was a solution, but the problem here was to find it in so short a time. Did I hear that correctly—that there's always a solution to a tangle like this?"

"There's always any number of solutions," Padma said. "The problem is to find the one you'd prefer—or maybe just the one you'd accept. Human situations, being human-made, are always mutable at human hands, if you can get to them with the proper pressures before they happen. Once they happen, of course, they become history—"

He smiled at me.

"—And history, so far at least, is something we aren't able to change. But changing what's about to happen simply requires getting to the base of the forces involved in time, with the right sort of pressures exerted in the right directions. What takes time is identifying the forces, finding what pressures are possible and where to apply them."

"And we don't have time."

His smile went.

"No. In fact, you don't."

I looked squarely at him.

"In that case, shouldn't you be thinking of leaving, yourself?" I said. "According to what I gather about these Naharese, once they overrun this place, they're liable to kill anyone they come across here. Aren't you too valuable to Mara to get your throat cut by some battle-drunk soldier?"

"I'd like to think so," he said. "But you see, from our point of view, what's happening here has importances that go entirely beyond the local, or even the planetary situation. Ontogenetics identifies certain individuals as possibly being particularly influential on the history of their time. Ontogenetics, of course, can be wrong—it's been wrong before this. But we think the value of studying such people as closely as possible at certain times is important enough to take priority over everything else."

"Historically influential? Do you mean William?" I said. "Who else—not the Conde? Someone in the revolutionary camp?"

Padma shook his head.

"If we tagged certain individuals publicly as being influential men and women of their historic time, we would only prejudice their actions and the actions of the people who knew them and muddle our own conclusions about them—even if we could be sure that ontogenetics had read their importance rightly; and we can't be sure."

"You don't get out of it that easily," I said. "The fact you're physically here probably means that the individuals you're watching are right here in Gebel

Nahar. I can't believe it's the Conde. His day is over, no matter how things go. That leaves the rest of us. Michael's a possibility, but he's deliberately chosen to bury himself. I know I'm not someone to shape history. Amanda? Kensie and Ian?"

He looked at me a little sadly.

"All of you, one way or another, have a hand in shaping history. But who shapes it largely, and who only a little is something I can't tell you. As I say, ontogenetics isn't that sure. As to whom I may be watching, I watch everyone."

It was a gentle, but impenetrable, shield he opposed me with. I let the matter go. I glanced out the window, but there was no sign of Ian.

"Maybe you can explain how Amanda, or you go about looking for a solution," I said.

"As I said, it's a matter of looking for the base of the existing forces at work—"

"The ranchers—and William?"

He nodded.

"Particularly William—since he's the prime mover. To get the results he wants, William or anyone else has to set up a structure of cause and effect, operating through individuals. So, for anyone else to control the forces already set to work, and bend them to different results, it's necessary to find where William's structure is vulnerable to cross-pressures and arrange for those to operate—again through individuals."

"And Amanda hasn't found a weak point yet?"

"Of course she has. Several." He frowned at me, but with a touch of humor. "I don't have any objection to telling you all this. You don't need to draw me with leading questions."

"Sorry," I said.

"It's all right. As I say, she's already found several. But none that can be implemented between now and sometime tomorrow, if the regiments attack Gebel Nahar then."

I had a strange sensation. As if a gate was slowly but inexorably being closed in my face.

"It seems to me," I said, "the easiest thing to change would be the position of the Conde. If he'd just agree to come to terms with the regiments, the whole thing would collapse."

"Obvious solutions are usually not the easiest," Padma said. "Stop and think. Why do you suppose the Conde would never change his mind?"

"He's a Naharese," I said. "More than that, he's honestly an hispanic. *El honor* forbids that he yield an inch to soldiers who were supposedly loyal to him and now are threatening to destroy him and everything he stands for."

"But tell me," said Padma, watching me. "Even if *el honor* was satisfied, would he want to treat with the rebels?"

I shook my head.

"No," I said. It was something I had recognized before this, but only with the back of my head. As I spoke to Padma now, it was like something emerging from the shadows to stand in the full light of day. "This is the great moment of his life. This is the chance for him to substantiate that paper title of his, to make it real. This way he can prove to himself he is a real aristocrat. He'd give his life—in fact, he can hardly wait to give his life—to win that."

There was a little silence.

"So you see," said Padma. "Go on, then. What other ways do you see a solution being found?"

"Ian and Kensie could void the contract and make the penalty payment. But they won't. Aside from the fact that no responsible officer from our world would risk giving the Dorsai the sort of bad name that could give, under these special circumstances, neither of those two brothers would abandon the Conde as long as he insisted on fighting. It's as impossible for a Dorsai to do that as it is for the Conde to play games with *el honor*. Like him, their whole life has been oriented against any such thing."

"What other ways?"

"I can't think of any," I said. "I'm out of suggestions—which is probably why I was never considered for anything like Amanda's job, in the first place."

"As a matter of fact, there are a number of other possible solutions," Padma said. His voice was soft, almost pedantic. "There's the possibility of bringing counter economic pressure upon William—but there's no time for that. There's also the possibility of bringing social and economic pressure upon the ranchers; and there's the possibility of disrupting the control of the revolutionaries who've come in from outside Nahar to run this rebellion. In each case, none of these solutions are of the kind that can very easily be made to work in the short time we've got."

"In fact, there isn't any such thing as a solution that can be made to work in time, isn't that right?" I said, bluntly.

He shook his head.

"No. Absolutely wrong. If we could stop the clock at this second and take the equivalent of some months to study the situation, we'd undoubtedly find not only one, but several solutions that would abort the attack of the regiments in the time we've got to work with. What you lack isn't time in which to act, since that's merely something specified for the solution. What you lack is time in which to discover the solution that will work in the time there is to act."

"So you mean," I said, "that we're to sit here tomorrow with Michael's forty or so bandsmen—and face the attack of something like six thousand line troops, even though they're only Naharese line troops, all the time knowing that there is absolutely a way in which that attack doesn't have to happen, if only we had the sense to find it?"

"The sense—and the time," said Padma. "But yes, you're right. It's a harsh reality of life, but the sort of reality that history has turned on, since history began."

"I see," I said. "Well, I find I don't accept it that easily."

"No." Padma's gaze was level and cooling upon me. "Neither does Amanda. Neither does Ian or Kensie. Nor, I suspect, even Michael. But then, you're all Dorsai."

I said nothing. It is a little embarrassing when someone plays your own top card against you.

"In any case," Padma went on, "none of you are being called on to merely accept it. Amanda's still at work. So is Ian, so are all the rest of you. Forgive me, I didn't mean to sneer at the reflexes of your culture. I envy you—a great many people envy you—that inability to give in. My point is that the fact that we know there's an answer makes no difference. You'd all be doing the same thing anyway, wouldn't you?"

"True enough," I said—and at that moment we were interrupted.

"Padma?" It was the general office annunciator speaking from the walls around us with Amanda's voice. "Could you give me some help, please?"

Padma got to his feet.

"I've got to go," he said.

He went out. I sat where I was, held by that odd little melancholy that had caught me up—and I think does the same with most Dorsai away from home—at moments all through my life. It is not a serious thing, just a touch of loneliness and sadness and the facing of the fact that life is measured; and there are only so

many things that can be accomplished in it, try how you may.

I was still in this mood when Ian's return to the office suite by the corridor door woke me out of it.

I got up.

"Corunna!" he said, and led the way into his private office. "How's the training going?"

"As you'd expect," I said. "I left Michael alone with them, at his suggestion. He thinks they might learn faster without my presence to distract them."

"Possible," said Ian.

He stepped to the window wall and looked out. My height was not enough to let me look over the edge of the parapet on this terrace and see down to the first where the bandsmen were drilling; but I guessed that his was.

"They don't seem to be doing badly," he said.

He was still on his feet, of course, and I was standing next to his desk. I looked at it now, and found the cube holding the image Amanda had talked about. The woman pictured there was obviously not Dorsai, but there was something not unlike our people about her. She was strong-boned and dark-haired, the hair sweeping down to her shoulders, longer than most Dorsais out in the field would have worn it, but not long according to the styles of Earth.

I looked back at Ian. He had turned away from the window and his contemplation of the drill going on two levels below. But he had stopped, part way in his backturn, and his face was turned toward the wall beyond which Amanda would be working with Padma at this moment. I saw him in three-quarter's face, with the light from the window wall striking that quarter of his features that was averted from me; and I noticed a tiredness about him. Not that it showed anywhere specifically in the lines of his face. He was, as always, like a mountain of granite, untouchable. But something about the way he stood spoke of a fatigue—perhaps a fatigue of the spirit rather than of the body.

"I just heard about Leah, here," I said, nodding at the image cube, speaking to bring him back to the moment.

He turned as if his thoughts had been a long way away.

"Leah? Oh, yes." His own eyes went absently to the cube and away again. "Yes, she's Earth. I'll be going to get her after this is over. We'll be married in two months."

"That soon?" I said. "I hadn't even heard you'd fallen in love."

"Love?" he said. His eyes were still on me, but their attention had gone away again. He spoke more as if to himself than to me. "No, it was years ago I fell in love. . ."

His attention focused, suddenly. He was back with me.

"Sit down," he said, dropping into the chair behind his desk. I sat. "Have you talked to Kensie since breakfast?"

"Just a little while ago, when I was asking around to find you," I said.

"He's got a couple of runs outside the walls he'd like your hand with, tonight after dark's well settled in."

"I know," I said. "He told me about them. A sweep of the slope in front of this place to clear it before laying mines there, and a scout of the regimental camp

for whatever we can learn about them before tomorrow."

"That's right," Ian said.

"Do you have any solid figures on how many there are out there?"

"Regimental rolls," said Ian, "give us a total of a little over five thousand of all ranks. Fifty-two hundred and some. But something like this invariably attracts a number of Naharese who scent personal glory, or at least the chance for personal glory. Then there're perhaps seven or eight hundred honest revolutionaries in Nahar, Padma estimates, individuals who've been working to loosen the grip of the rancher oligarchy for

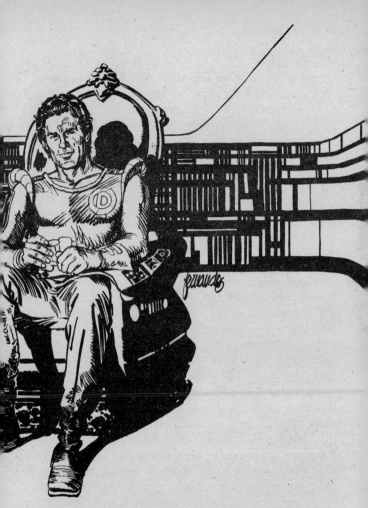

some time. Plus a hundred or so agents provocateurs from outside.''

"In something like this, those who aren't trained soldiers we can probably discount, don't you think?''

Ian nodded.

"How many of the actual soldiers'll have had any actual combat experience?" I asked.

"Combat experience in this part of Ceta," Ian said, "means having been involved in a border clash or two with the armed forces of the surrounding principalities. Maybe one in ten of the line soldiers has had that. On the other hand, every male, particularly in Nahar, has dreamed of a dramatic moment like this."

"So they'll all come on hard with the first attack," I said.

"That's as I see it," said Ian, "and Kensie agrees. I'm glad to hear it's your thought, too. Everyone out there will attack in that first charge, not merely determined to do well, but dreaming of outdoing everyone else around him. If we can throw them back even once, some of them won't come again. And that's the way it ought to go. They won't lose heart as a group. Just each setback will take the heart out of some, and we'll work them down to the hard core that's serious about being willing to die if only they can get over the walls and reach us."

"Yes," I said, "and how many of those do you think there are?"

"That's the problem," said Ian, calmly. "At the very least, there's going to be one in fifty we'll have to kill to stop. Even if half of them are already out by the time we get down to it, that's sixty of them left; and we've got to figure by that time we'll have taken at least thirty percent casualties ourselves—and that's an optimistic figure, considering the fact that these bandsmen are next thing to noncombatants. Man to man, on the kind of hardcore attackers that are going to be making it over the walls, the bandsmen that're left will be lucky to take care of an equal number of attackers. Padma, of course, doesn't exist in our defensive table of personnel. That leaves you, me, Kensie, Michael, and Amanda to handle about thirty bodies. Have you been keeping yourself in condition?"

I grinned.

"That's good," said Ian. "I forgot to figure that scar-face of yours. Be sure to smile like that when they come at you. It ought to slow them down for a couple of seconds at least, and we'll need all the help we can get."

I laughed.

"If Michael doesn't want you, how about working with Kensie for the rest of the afternoon?"

"Fine," I said.

I got up and went out. Kensie looked up from his printouts when he saw me again.

"Find him?" he asked.

"Yes. He suggested you could use me."

"I can. Join me."

We worked together the rest of the afternoon. The so-called large scale terrain maps the Naharese army library provided were hardly more useful than tourist brochures from our point of view. What Kensie needed to know was what the ground was like meter by meter from the front walls on out over perhaps a couple of hundred meters of plain beyond where the slope of the mountain met it. Given that knowledge, it would be possible to make reasonable estimates as to how a foot attack might develop, how many attackers we might be likely to have on a front, and on which parts of that front, because of vegetation, or the footing or the terrain, attackers might be expected to fall behind their fellows during a rush.

The Naharese terrain maps had never been made with such a detailed information of the ground in mind. To correct them, Kensie had spent most of the day before taking telescopic pictures of three-meter square segments of the ground, using the watch cameras built into the ramparts of the first wall. With these pictures as reference, we now proceeded to make notes on blown-up versions of the clumsy Naharese maps.

It took us the rest of the afternoon; but by the time we were finished, we had a fairly good working knowledge of the ground before the Gebel Nahar, from the viewpoint not only of someone storming up it, but from the viewpoint of a defender who might have to cover it on his belly—as Kensie and I would be doing that night. We knocked off, with the job done, finally, about the dinner hour.

In spite of having finished at a reasonable time, we found no one else at dinner but Ian. Michael was still up to his ears in the effort of teaching his bandsmen to be fighting troops; and Amanda was still with Padma, hard at the search for a solution, even at this eleventh hour.

"You'd both probably better get an hour of sleep, if you can spare the time," Ian said to me. "We might be able to pick up an hour or two more of rest just before dawn, but there's no counting on it."

"Yes," said Kensie. "And you might grab some sleep, yourself."

Brother looked at brother. They knew each other so well, they were so complete in their understanding of each other, that neither one bothered to discuss the matter further. It had been discussed silently in that one momentary exchange of glances, and now they were concerned with other things.

As it turned out, I was able to get a full three hours of sleep. It was just after ten o'clock, local time when Kensie and I came out from Gebel Nahar. On the reasonable assumption that the regiments would have watchers keeping an eye on our walls—that same watch Kensie and I were to silence so that the bandsmen could mine the slope—I had guessed we would be doing something like going out over a dark portion of the front wall on a rope. Instead, Michael was to lead us, properly outfitted and with our face

and hands blackened, through some cellarways and along a passage that would let us out into the night a good fifty meters beyond the wall.

"How did you know about this?" I asked, as he took us along the passage. "If there's more secret ways like this, and the regiments know about them—"

"There aren't and they don't," said Michael. We were going almost single file down the concrete-walled tunnel as he answered me. "This is a private escape hatch that's the secret of the Conde, and no one else. His father had it built thirty-eight local years ago. Our Conde called me in to tell me about it when he heard the regiments had deserted."

122

I nodded. There was plainly a sympathy and a friendship between Michael and the old Conde that I had not had time to ask about. Perhaps it had come of their each being the only one of their kind in Gebel Nahar.

We reached the end of the tunnel and the foot of a short wooden ladder leading up to a circular metal hatch. Michael turned out the light in the tunnel and we were suddenly in absolute darkness. I heard him cranking something well-oiled, for it turned almost noiselessly. Above us the circular hatch lifted slowly to show starlit sky.

"Go ahead," Michael whispered. "Keep your heads

down. The bushes that hide this spot have thorns at the end of their leaves."

We went up; I led, as being the more expendable of the two of us. The thorns did not stab me, although I heard them scratch against the stiff fabric of the black combat overalls I was wearing, as I pushed my way through the bushes, keeping level to the ground. I heard Kensie come up behind me and the faint sound of the hatch being closed behind us. Michael was due to open it again in two hours and fourteen minutes.

Kensie touched my shoulder. I looked and saw his hand held up, to silhouette itself against the stars. He made the hand signal for *move out,* touched me again lightly on the shoulder and disappeared. I turned away and began to move off in the opposite direction, staying close to the ground.

I had forgotten what a sweep like this was like. As with all our people, I had been raised with the idea of being always in effective physical condition. Of course, in itself, this is almost a universal idea nowadays. Most cultures emphasize keeping the physical vehicle in shape so as to be able to deliver the mental skills wherever the market may require them. But, because in our case the conditions of our work are so physically demanding, we have probably placed more emphasis on it. It has become an idea which begins in the cradle and becomes almost an ingrained reflex, like washing or brushing teeth.

This may be one of the reasons we have so many people living to advanced old age; apart from those naturally young for their years like the individuals in Amanda's family. Certainly, I think, it is one of the reasons why we tend to be active into extreme old age, right up to the moment of death. But, with the best efforts possible, even our training does not produce the same results as practice.

Ian had been right to needle me about my condition, gently as he had done it. The best facilities aboard the biggest space warships do not compare to the reality of being out in the field. My choice of work lies between the stars, but there is no denying that those like myself who spend the working years in ships grow rusty in the area of ordinary body skills. Now, at night, out next to the earth on my own, I could feel a sort of self-consciousness of my body. I was too aware of the weight of my flesh and bones, the effort my muscles made, and the awkwardness of the creeping and crawling positions in which I had to cover the ground.

I worked to the right as Kensie was working left, covering the slope segment by segment, clicking off these chunks of Cetan surface in my mind according to the memory pattern in which I had fixed them. It was all sand and gravel and low brush, most with built-in defenses in the form of thorns or burrs. The night wind blew like an invisible current around me in the darkness, cooling me under a sky where no clouds hid the stars.

The light of a moon would have been welcome, but Ceta has none. After about fifteen minutes I came to the first of nine positions that we had marked in my area as possible locations for watchers from the enemy camp. Picking such positions is a matter of simple reasoning. Anyone but the best trained of observers, given the job of watching something like the Gebel Nahar, from which no action is really expected to develop, would find the hours long. Particularly, when the

hours in question are cool nighttime hours out in the middle of a plain where there is little to occupy the attention. Under those conditions, the watcher's certainty that he is simply putting in time grows steadily; and with the animal instinct in him he drifts automatically to the most comfortable or sheltered location from which to do his watching.

But there was no one at the first of the positions I came to. I moved on.

It was just about this time that I began to be aware of a change in the way I was feeling. The exercise, the

adjustment of my body to the darkness and the night temperature, had begun to have their effects. I was no longer physically self-conscious. Instead, I was beginning to enjoy the action.

Old habits and reflexes had awakened in me. I flowed over the ground, now, not an intruder in the night of Nahar, but part of it. My eyes had adjusted to the dim illumination of the starlight, and I had the illusion that I was seeing almost as well as I might have in the day.

Just so, with my hearing. What had been a confusion of dark sounds had separated and identified itself as a multitude of different auditory messages. I heard the wind in the bushes without confusing it with the distant noise-making of some small, wild plains animal. I smelled the different and separate odors of the vegetation. Now I was able to hold the small sounds of my own passage—the scuff of my hands and body upon the ground—separate from the other noises that rode the steady stream of the breeze. In the end, I was not only aware of them all, I was aware of being one with them—one of the denizens of the Cetan night.

There was an excitement to it, a feeling of naturalness and rightness in my quiet search through this dim-lit land. I felt not only at home here, but as if in some measure I owned the night. The wind, the scents, the sounds I heard, all entered into me; and I recognized suddenly that I had moved completely beyond an awareness of myself as a physical body separate from what surrounded me. I was pure observer, with the keen involvement that a wild animal feels in the world he moves through. I was disembodied; a pair of eyes, a nose and two ears, sweeping invisibly through the world. I had forgotten Gebel Nahar. I had almost forgotten to think like a human. Almost—for a few moments—I had forgotten Else.

Then a sense of duty came and hauled me back to my obligations. I finished my sweep. There were no observers at all, either at any of the likely positions Kensie and I had picked out or anywhere else in the area I had covered. Unbelievable as it seemed from a military standpoint, the regiments had not even bothered to keep a token watch on us. For a second I wondered if they had never had any intention at all of at-

tacking, as Ian had believed they would; and as everyone else, including the Conde and Michael's bandsmen, had taken for granted.

I returned to the location of the the tunnel-end, and met Kensie there. His hand-signal showed that he had also found his area deserted. There was no reason why Michael's men should not be moved out as soon as possible and put to work laying the mines.

Michael opened the hatch at the scheduled time and we went down the ladder by feel in the darkness. With the hatch once more closed overhead, the light came on again.

"What did you find?" Michael asked, as we stood squinting in the glare.

"Nothing," said Kensie. "It seems they're ignoring us. You've got the mines ready to go?"

"Yes," said Michael. "If it's safe out there, do you want to send the men out by one of the regular gates? I promised the Conde to keep the secret of this tunnel."

"Absolutely," said Kensie. "In any case, the less people who know about this sort of way in and out of a place like Gebel Nahar, the better. Let's go back inside and get things organized."

We went. Back in Kensie's office, we were joined by Amanda, who had temporarily put aside her search for a social solution to the situation. We sat around in a circle and Kensie and I reported on what we had found.

"The thought occurred to me," I said, "that something might have come up to change the mind of the Naharese about attacking here."

Kensie and Ian shook their heads so unanimously

and immediately it was as if they had reacted by instinct. The small hope in the back of my mind flickered and died. Experienced as the two of them were, if they were that certain, there was little room for doubt.

"I haven't waked the men yet," said Michael, "because after that drill on the weapons today they needed all the sleep they could get. I'll call the orderly and tell him to wake them now. We can be outside and at work in half an hour; and except for my rotating them in by groups for food and rest breaks, we can work straight through the night. We ought to have all the mines placed by a little before dawn."

"Good," said Ian.

I sat watching him, and the others. My sensations, outside of having become one with the night, had left my senses keyed to an abnormally sharp pitch. I was feeling now like a wild animal brought into the artificial world of indoors. The lights overhead in the office seemed harshly bright. The air itself was full of alien, mechanical scents, little trace odors carried on the ventilating system of oil and room dust, plus all the human smells that result when our race is cooped up within a structure.

And part of this sensitivity was directed toward the other four people in the room. It seemed to me that I saw, heard and smelled them with an almost painful acuity. I read the way each of them was feeling to a degree I had never been able to, before.

They were all deadly tired—each in his or her own way, very tired, with a personal, inner exhaustion that had finally been exposed by the physical tiredness to which the present situation had brought all of them except me. It seemed what that physical tiredness had

accomplished had been to strip away the polite covering that before had hidden the private exhaustion; and
it was now plain on every one of them.

"...Then there's no reason for the rest of us to
waste any more time," Ian was saying. "Amanda, you
and I'd better dress and equip for that scout of their
camp. Knife and sidearm, only."

His words brought me suddenly out of my separate
awareness.

"You and Amanda?" I said. "I thought it was
Kensie and I, Michael and Amanda who were going to
take a look at the camp?"

"It was," said Ian. "One of the Governors who

came in to talk to us yesterday is on his way in by personal aircraft. He wants to talk to Kensie again, privately—he won't talk to anyone else."

"Some kind of a deal in the offing?"

"Possibly," said Kensie. "We can't count on it, though, so we go ahead. On the other hand we can't ignore the chance. So I'll stay and Ian will go."

"We could do it with three," I said.

"Not as well as it could be done by four," said Ian. "That's a good-sized camp to get into and look over in a hurry. If anyone but Dorsai could be trusted to get in and out without being seen, I'd be glad to take half a dozen more. It's not like most military camps, where there's a single overall headquarters area. We're going to have to check the headquarters of each regiment; and there're six of them."

I nodded.

"You'd better get something to eat, Corunna," Ian went on. "We could be out until dawn."

It was good advice. When I came back from eating, the other three who were to go were already in Ian's office, and outfitted. On his right thigh Michael was wearing a knife—which was after all, more tool than weapon—but he wore no sidearms and I noticed Ian did not object. With her hands and face blacked, wearing the black stocking cap, overalls and boots, Amanda looked taller and more square-shouldered than she had in her daily clothes.

"All right," said Ian. He had the plan of the camp laid out, according to our telescopic observation of it through the rampart watch-cameras, combined with what Michael had been able to tell us of Naharese habits.

"We'll go by field experience," he said. "I'll take two of the six regiments—the two in the center. Michael, because he's more recently from his Academy training and because he knows these people, will take two regiments—the two on the left wing that includes the far left one that was his own Third Regiment. You'll take the Second Regiment, Corunna, and Amanda will take the Fourth. I mention this now in case we don't have a chance to talk outside the camp."

"It's unlucky you and Michael can't take regiments adjoining each other," I said. "That'd give you a chance to work together. You might need that with two regiments apiece to cover."

"Ian needs to see the Fifth Regiment for himself, if possible," Michael said. "That's the Guard Regiment, the one with the best arms. And since my regiment is a traditional enemy of the Guard Regiment, the two have deliberately been separated as far as possible— that's why the Guards are in the middle and my Third's on the wing."

"Anything else? Then we should go," said Ian.

We went out quietly by the same tunnel by which Kensie and I had gone for our sweep of the slope, leaving the hatch propped a little open against our return. Once in the open we spread apart at about a ten meter interval and began to jog toward the lights of the regimental camp, in the distance.

We were a little over an hour coming up on it. We began to hear it when we were still some distance from it. It did not resemble a military camp on the eve of battle half so much as it did a large open-air party.

The camp was laid out in a crescent. The center of each regimental area was made up of the usual

beehive-shaped buildings of blown bubble-plastic that could be erected so easily on the spot. Behind and between the clumpings of these were ordinary tents of all types and sizes. There was noise and steady traffic between these tents and the plastic buildings as well as between the plastic buildings themselves.

We stopped a hundred meters out, opposite the center of the crescent and checked off. We were able to stand talking, quite openly. Even if we had been without our black accoutrements, the general sound and activity going on just before us ensured as much privacy and protection as a wall between us and the camp would have afforded.

"All back here in forty minutes," Ian said.

We checked chronometers and split up, going in. My target, the Second Regiment, was between Ian's two regiments and Michael's Two; and it was a section that had few tents, these seeming to cluster most thickly either toward the center of the camp or out on both wings. I slipped between the first line of buildings, moving from shadow to shadow. It was foolishly easy. Even if I had not already loosened myself up on the scout across the slope before Gebel Nahar, I would have found it easy. It was very clear that even if I had come, not in scouting blacks but wearing ordinary local clothing and obviously mispronouncing the local Spanish accent, I could have strolled freely and openly wherever I wanted. Individuals in all sorts of civilian clothing were intermingled with the uniformed military; and it became plain almost immediately that few of the civilians were known by name and face to the soldiers. Ironically, my night battle dress was the one outfit that would have attracted unwelcome attention

—if they had noticed me.

But there was no danger that they would notice me. Effectively, the people moving between the buildings and among the tents had neither eyes nor ears for what was not directly under their noses. Getting about unseen under such conditions boils down simply to the fact that you move quietly—which means moving all of you in a single rhythm, including your breathing; and that when you stop, you become utterly still—which means being completely relaxed in whatever bodily position you have stopped in.

Breathing is the key to both, of course, as we learn back home in childhood games even before we are school age. Move in rhythm and stop utterly and you can sometimes stand in plain sight of someone who does not expect you to be there, and go unobserved. How many times has everyone had the experience of being looked "right through" by someone who does not expect to see them at a particular place or moment?

So, there was no difficulty in what I had to do; and as I say, my experience on the slope had already keyed me. I fell back into my earlier feeling of being nothing but senses—eyes, ears, and nose, drifting invisibly through the scenes of the Naharese camp. A quick circuit of my area told me all we needed to know about this particular regiment.

Most of the soldiers were between late twenties and early forties in age. Under other conditions this might have meant a force of veterans. In this case, it indicated just the opposite, time-servers who liked the uniform, the relatively easy work, and the authority and freedom of being in the military. I found a few

field energy weapons—light, three-man pieces that were not only out-of-date, but impractical to bring into action in open territory like that before Gebel Nahar. The heavier weapons we had emplaced on the ramparts would be able to take out such as these almost as soon as the rebels could try to put them into action, and long before they could do any real damage to the heavy defensive walls.

The hand weapons varied, ranging from the best of newer energy guns, cone rifles and needle guns—in the hands of the soldiers—to the strangest assortment of ancient and modern hunting tools and slug-throwing sport pieces—carried by those in civilian clothing. I did not see any crossbows or swords; but it would not have surprised me if I had. The civilian and the military hand weapons alike, however, had one thing in common that surprised me, in the light of everything else I saw—they were clean, well-cared for, and handled with respect.

I decided I had found out as much as necessary about this part of the camp. I headed back to the first row of plastic structures and the darkness of the plains beyond, having to detour slightly to avoid a drunken brawl that had spilled out of one of the buildings into the space between it and the next. In fact, there seemed to be a good deal of drinking and drugging going on, although none of those I saw had got themselves to the edge of unconsciousness yet.

It was on this detour that I became conscious of someone quietly moving parallel to me. In this place and time, it was highly unlikely that there was anyone who could do so with any secrecy and skill except one of us who had come out from Gebel Nahar. Since it was on the side of my segment that touched the area given to Michael to investigate, I guessed it was he. I went to look, and found him.

I've got something to show you, he hand signalled me. *Are you done, here?*

Yes, I told him.

Come on, then.

He led me into his area, to one of the larger plastic buildings in the territory of the second regiment he had been given to investigate. He brought me to the building's back. The curving sides of such structures are not difficult to climb quietly if you have had some practise doing so. He led me to the top of the roof curve and pointed at a small hole.

I looked in and saw six men with the collar tabs of Regimental Commanders, sitting together at a table, apparently having sometime since finished a meal. Also present were some officers of lesser rank, but none of these were at the table. Bubble plastic, in addition to its other virtues, is a good sound baffle; and since the table and those about it were not directly under the observation hole, but over against one of the curving walls, some distance off, I could not make out their conversation. It was just below comprehension level. I could hear their words, but not understand them.

But I could watch the way they spoke and their gestures, and tell how they were reacting to each other. It became evident, after a few minutes, that there were a great many tensions around that table. There was no open argument, but they sat and looked at each other in ways that were next to open challenges and the rumble of their voices bristled with the electricity of controlled angers.

I felt my shoulder tapped, and took my attention from the hole to the night outside. It took a few seconds to adjust to the relative darkness on top of the structure; but when I did, I could see the Michael was again talking to me with his hands.

Look at the youngest of the Commanders—the one on your left, with the very black mustache. That's the Commander of my regiment.

I looked, identified the man, and lifted my gaze from the hole briefly to nod.

Now look across the table and as far down from him as possible. You see the somewhat heavy Commander with the gray sideburns and the lips that almost pout?

I looked, raised my head and nodded again.

That's the Commander of the Guard Regiment. He and my Commander are beginning to wear on each other. If not, they'd be seated side by side and pretending that anything that ever was between their two regiments has been put aside. It's almost as bad with the junior officers, if you know the signs to look for in each one's case. Can you guess what's triggered it off?

No, I told him, *but I suppose you do, or you wouldn't have brought me here.*

I've been watching for some time. They had the maps out earlier, and it was easy to tell what they were discussing. It's the position of each regiment in the line of battle, tomorrow. They've agreed what it's to be, at last, but no one's happy with the final decision.

I nodded.

I wanted you to see it for yourself. They're all ready to go at each other's throats and it's an explosive situation. Maybe Amanda can find something in it she can use. I brought you here because I was hoping that when we go back to rendezvous with the others, you'll support me in suggesting she come and see this for herself.

I nodded again. The brittle emotions betrayed by the commanders below had been obvious, even to me, the moment I had first looked through the hole.

We slipped quietly back down the curve of the building to the shadowed ground at its back and moved out together toward the rendezvous point.

We had no trouble making our way out through the rest of the encampment and back to our meeting spot. It was safely beyond the illumination of the lights that the regiments had set up amongst their buildings. Ian and Amanda were already there; and we stood together, looking back at the activity in the encampment as we compared notes.

"I called Captain El Man in to look at something I'd found," Michael said. "In my alternate area, there was a meeting going on between the regimental commanders—"

The sound of a shot from someone's antique explosive firearm cut him short. We all turned toward the encampment; and saw a lean figure wearing a white shirt brilliantly reflective in the lights, running toward us, while a gang of men poured out of one of the tents, stared about, and then started in pursuit.

The one they chased was running directly for us, in his obvious desire to get away from the camp. It would have been easy to believe that he had seen us and was running to us for help; but the situation did not support that conclusion. Aside from the unlikeliness of his seeking aid from strangers dressed and equipped as we were, it was obvious that with his eyes still dilated from the lights of the camp, and staring at black-dressed figures like ours, he was completely unable to see us.

All of us dropped flat into the sparse grass of the

plain. But he still came straight for us. Another shot sounded from his pursuers.

It only seems, of course, that the luck in such situations is always bad. It is not so, of course. Good and bad balance out. But knowing this does not help when things seem freakishly determined to do their worst. The fugitive had all the open Naharese plain into which to run. He came toward us instead as if drawn on a cable. We lay still. Unless he actually stepped on one of us, there was a chance he could run right through us and not know we were there.

He did not step on one of us, but he did trip over Michael, stagger on a step, check, and glance down to see what had interrupted his flight. He looked directly at Amanda, and stopped, staring down in astonishment. A second later, he had started to swing around to face his pursuers, his mouth open to shout to them.

Whether he had expected the information of what he had found to soothe their anger toward him, or whether he had simply forgotten at that moment that they had been chasing him, was beside the point. He was obviously about to betray our presence, and Amanda did exactly the correct thing—even if it produced the least desirable results. She uncoiled from the ground like a spring released from tension, one fist taking the fugitive in the adam's apple to cut off his cry and the other going into him just under the breastbone to take the wind out of him and put him down without killing him.

She had been forced to rise between him and his pursuers. But, all black as she was in contrast to the brilliant whiteness of his shirt, she would well have flickered for a second before their eyes without being

recognized; and with the man down, we could have slipped away from the pursuers without their realizing until too late that we had been there. But the incredible bad luck of that moment was still with us.

As she took the man down, another shot sounded from the pursuers, clearly aimed at the now-stationary target of the fugitive—and Amanda went down with him.

She was up again in a second.

"Fine—I'm fine," she said. "Let's go!"

We went, fading off into the darkness at the same steady trot at which we had come to the camp. Until we were aware of specific pursuit there was no point in burning up our reserves of energy. We moved steadily away, back toward Gebel Nahar, while the pursuers finally reached the fugitive, surrounded him, got him on his feet and talking.

By that time we could see them flashing around them the lights some of them had been carrying, searching the plain for us. But we were well away by that time, and drawing farther off every second. No pursuit developed.

"Too bad," said Ian, as the sound and lights of the camp dwindled behind us. "But no great harm done. What happened to you, 'Manda?"

She did not answer. Instead, she went down again, stumbling and dropping abruptly. In a second we were all back and squatting around her.

She was plainly having trouble breathing.

"Sorry. . ." she whispered.

Ian was already cutting away the clothing over her left shoulder.

"Not much blood," he said.

The tone of his voice said he was very angry with her. So was I. It was entirely possible that she might have killed herself by trying to run with a wound that should not have been excited by that kind of treatment. She had acted instinctively to hide the knowledge that she had been hit by that last shot, so that the rest of us would not hesitate in getting away safely. It was not hard to understand the impulse that had made her do it—but she should not have.

"Corunna," said Ian, moving aside. "This is more in your line."

He was right. As a captain, I was the closest thing to a physician aboard, most of the time. I moved in beside her and checked the wound as best I could. In the general but faint starlight it showed as merely a small patch of darkness against a larger, pale patch of exposed flesh. I felt it with my fingers and put my cheek down against it.

"Small caliber slug," I said. Ian breathed a little harshly out through his nostrils. He had already deduced that much. I went on. "Not a sucking wound. High up, just below the collarbone. No immediate pneumothorax, but the chest cavity'll be filling with blood. Are you very short of breath, Amanda? Don't talk, just nod or shake your head."

She nodded.

"How do you feel. Dizzy? Faint?"

She nodded again. Her skin was clammy to my touch.

"Going into shock," I said.

I put my ear to her chest again.

"Right," I said. "The lung on this side's not filling with air. She can't run. She shouldn't do anything.

We'll need to carry her."

"I'll do that," said Ian. He was still angry—irrationally, emotionally angry, but trying to control it. "How fast do we have to get her back, do you think?"

"Her condition ought to stay the same for a couple of hours," I said. "Looks like no large blood vessels were hit; and the smaller vessels tend to be self-sealing. But the pleural cavity on this side has been filling up with blood and she's collapsed a lung. That's why she's having trouble breathing. No blood around her mouth, so it probably didn't nick an airway going through. . ."

I felt around behind her shoulder but found no exit wound.

"It didn't go through. If there're MASH med-mech units back at Gebel Nahar and we get her back in the next two hours, she should be all right—if we carry her."

Ian scooped her into his arms. He stood up.

"Head down," I said.

"Right," he answered and put her over one shoulder in a fireman's carry. "No, wait—we'll need some padding for my shoulder."

Michael and I took off our jerseys and made a pad for his other shoulder. He transferred her to that shoulder, with her head hanging down his back. I sympathized with her. Even with the padding, it was not a comfortable way to travel; and her wound and shortness of breath would make it a great deal worse.

"Try it at a slow walk, first," I said.

"I'll try it. But we can't go slow walk all the way," said Ian. "It's nearly three klicks from where we are now."

He was right, of course. To walk her back over a distance of three kilometers would take too long. I went behind him to watch her as well as could be done. The sooner I got her to a med-mech unit the better. We started off, and he gradually increased his pace until we were moving smoothly but briskly.

"How are you?" he asked her, over his shoulder.

"She nodded," I reported, from my position behind him.

"Good," he said, and began to jog.

We travelled. She made no effort to speak, and none of the rest of us spoke. From time to time I moved up closer behind Ian to watch her at close range; and as far as I could tell, she did not lose consciousness once on that long, jolting ride; Ian forged ahead, something made of steel rather than of ordinary human flesh, his gaze fixed on the lights of Gebel Nahar, far off across the plain.

There is something that happens under those conditions where the choice is either to count the seconds, or disregard time altogether. In the end we all—and I think Amanda, too, as far as she was capable of controlling how she felt—went off a little way from ordinary time, and did not come back to it until we were at the entrance to the Conde's secret tunnel, leading back under the walls of Gebel Nahar.

By the time I got Amanda laid out in the medical section of Gebel Nahar, she looked very bad indeed and was only semi-conscious. Anything else, of course, would have been surprising indeed. It does not improve the looks of even a very healthy person to be carried head down for over thirty minutes. Luckily, the medical section had everything necessary in the way of med-mechs. I was able to find a portable unit that could be rigged for bed rest—vacuum pump, power unit, drainage bag. It was a matter of inserting a tube between Amanda's lung and chest wall—and this I left to the med-mech, which was less liable to human mistakes than I was on a day in which luck seemed to be running so badly—so that the unit could exhaust the blood from the pleural space into which it had drained.

It was also necessary to rig a unit to supply her with

reconstituted whole blood while this draining process was going on. However, none of this was difficult, even for a part-trained person like myself, once we got her safely to the medical section. I finally got her fixed up and left her to rest—she was in no shape to do much else.

I went off to the offices to find Ian and Kensie. They were both there; and they listened without interrupting to my report on Amanda's treatment and my estimate of her condition.

"She should rest for the next few days, I take it," said Ian when I was done.

"That's right," I said.

"There ought to be some way we could get her out of here, to safety and a regular hospital," said Kensie.

"How?" I asked. "It's almost dawn now. The Naharese would zero in on any vehicle that tried to leave this place, by ground or air. It'd never get away."

Kensie nodded soberly.

"They should," said Ian, "be starting to move now, if this dawn was to be the attack moment."

He turned to the window, and Kensie and I turned with him. Dawn was just breaking. The sky overhead was white-blue and hard, and the brown stretch of the plain looked also stony and hard and empty between the Gebel Nahar and the distant line of the encampment. It was very obvious, even without vision amplification, that the soldiers and others in the encampment had not even begun to form up in battle positions, let alone begin to move toward us.

"After all their parties last night, they may not get going until noon," I said.

"I don't think they'll be that late," said Ian, absent-

155

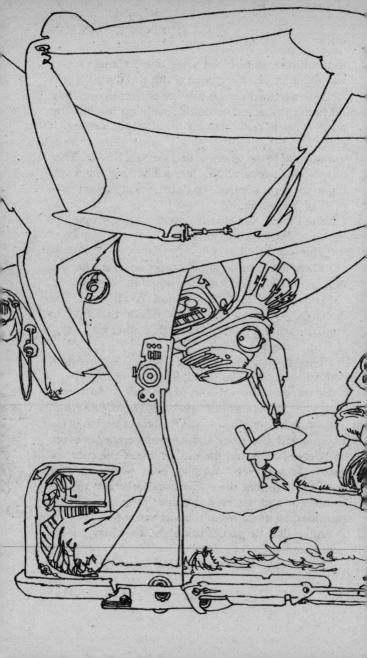

ly. He had taken me seriously. "At any rate, it gives us a little more time. Are you going to have to stay with Amanda?"

"I'll want to look in on her from time to time—in fact, I'm going back down now," I said. "I just came up to tell you how she is. But in between visits, I can be useful."

"Good," said Ian. "As soon as you've had another look at her, why don't you go see if you can help Michael. He's been saying he's got his doubts about those bandsmen of his."

"All right." I went out.

When I got back to the medical section, Amanda was asleep. I was going to slip out and leave her to rest, when she woke and recognized me.

"Corunna," she said, "how am I?"

"You're fine," I said, going back to the side of the bed where she lay. "All you need now is to get a lot of sleep and do a good job of healing."

"What's the situation outside?" she said. "Is it day, yet?"

We were in one of the windowless rooms in the interior of Gebel Nahar.

"Just dawn," I said. "Nothing happening so far. In any case, you forget about all that and rest."

"You'll need me up there."

"Not with a tube between your ribs," I said. "Lie back and sleep."

Her head moved restlessly on the pillow.

"It might have been better if that slug had been more on target."

I looked down at her.

"According to what I've heard about you," I said,

"you of all people ought to know that when you're in a hospital bed it's not the best time in the world to be worrying over things."

She started to speak, interrupted herself to cough, and was silent for a little time until the pain of the tube, rubbing inside her with the disturbance of her coughing, subsided. Even a deep breath would move that tube now, and pain her. There was nothing to be done about that, but I could see how shallowly she breathed, accordingly.

"No," she said. "I can't want to die. But the situation as it stands, is impossible; and every way out of it there is, is impossible, for all three of us. Just like our situation here in Gebel Nahar with no way out."

"Kensie and Ian are able to make up their own minds."

"It's not a matter of making up minds. It's a matter of impossibilities."

"Well," I said, "is there anything you can do about that?"

"I ought to be able to."

"Ought to, maybe, but can you?"

She breathed shallowly. Slowly she shook her head on the pillow.

"Then let it go. Leave it alone," I said. "I'll be back to check on you from time to time. Wait and see what develops."

"How can I wait?" she said. "I'm afraid of myself. Afraid I might throw everything overboard and do what I want most—and so ruin everyone."

"You won't do that."

"I might."

"You're exhausted," I told her. "You're in pain.

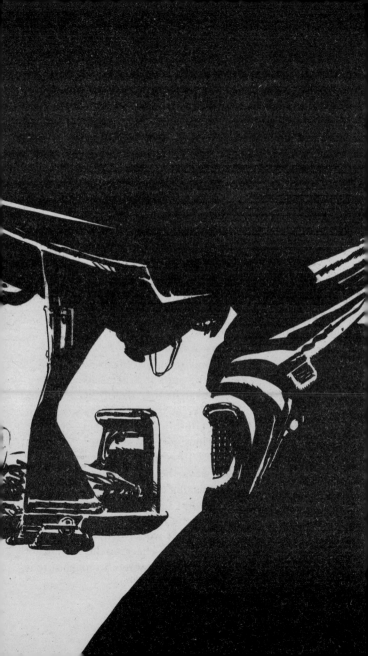

Stop trying to think. I'll be back in an hour or two to check on you. Until then, rest!"

I went out.

I took the corridors that led me to the band section. I saw no other bandsmen in the corridors as I approached their section, but an orderly was on duty as usual in Michael's outer office and Michael himself was in his own office, standing beside his desk with a sheaf of printed records in hand.

"Captain!" he said, when he saw me.

"I've got to look in on Amanda from time to time," I said. "But in between, Ian suggested you might find me useful."

"I'd always find you useful, sir," he said, with the ghost of a smile. "Do you want to come along to stores with me? I need to check a few items of supply and we can talk as we go."

"Of course."

We left the offices and he led me down other corridors and into a supply section. What he was after, it developed, was not the supplies themselves, but the automated delivery system that would keep feeding them, on command—or at regular intervals, without command, if the communications network was knocked out—to various sections of Gebel Nahar. It was a system of a sort I had never seen before.

"Another of the ways the ranchers who designed this looked ahead to having to hole up here," Michael explained as we looked at the supply bins for each of the various sections of the fortress, each bin already stocked with the supplies it would deliver as needed. He was going from bin to bin, checking the contents of each and testing each delivery system to make sure it was working.

The overhead lights were very bright, and their illumination reflected off solid concrete walls painted a utilitarian, flat white. The effect was both blinding and bleak at once; and the feeling of bleakness was reinforced by the stillness of the air. The ventilators must have been working here as in other interior parts of the Gebel Nahar, but with the large open space of the supply section and its high ceilings, the air felt as if there was no movement to it at all.

"Lucky for us," I said.

Michael nodded.

"Yes, if ever a place was made to be defended by a handful of people, this is it. Only, they didn't expect the defense to be by such a small handful as we are. They were thinking in terms of a hundred families, with servants and retainers. Still, if it comes to a last stand for us in the inner fort, on the top three levels, they're going to have to pay one hell of a price to get at us."

I watched his face as he worked. There was no doubt about it. He looked much more tired, much leaner, and older than he had appeared to me only a few days before when he had met Amanda and me at the spaceport terminal of Nahar City. But the work he had been doing and what he had gone through could not alone have been enough to cut him down so visibly, at his age.

He finished checking the last of the delivery systems and the last of the bins. He turned away.

"Ian tells me you've got some concern as to how your bandsmen may stand up to the attack," I said.

His mouth thinned and straightened.

"Yes," he said. There was a little pause, and then he added: "You can't blame them. If they'd been real soldier types they would have been in one of the line companies. There's security, but no chance of promotion to speak of, in a band."

Then humor came back to him, a tired but real smile.

"Of course, for someone like myself," he said, "that's ideal."

"On the other hand," I said. "They're here with us. They stayed."

"Well. . ." He sat down a little heavily on a short stack of boxes and waved me to another, "so far it hasn't cost them anything but some hard work. And they've been paid off in excitement. I think I said something to you about that when we were flying out from Nahar City. Excitement—drama—is what most Naharese live for; and die for, for that matter, if the drama is big enough."

"You don't think they'll fight when the time comes?"

"I don't know." His face was bleak again. "I only know I can't blame them—I can't, of all people—if they don't."

"Your attitude's a matter of conviction."

"Maybe theirs is, too. There's no way to judge any one person by another. You never know enough to make a real comparison."

"True," I said. "But I still think that if they don't fight, it'll be for somewhat lesser reasons than yours for not fighting."

He shook his head slowly.

"Maybe I'm wrong, all wrong." His tone was

almost bitter. "But I can't get outside myself to look at it. I only know I'm afraid."

"Afraid?" I looked at him. "Of fighting?"

"I wish it was of fighting," he laughed, briefly. "No, I'm afraid that I don't have the will *not* to fight. I'm afraid that at the last moment it'll all come back, all those early dreams and all the growing up and all the training—and I'll find myself killing, even though I'll know that it won't make any difference in the end and that the Naharese will take Gebel Nahar anyway."

"I don't think it'd be Gebel Nahar you'd be fighting for," I said slowly. "I think it'd be out of a natural, normal instinct to stay alive yourself as long as you can —or to help protect those who are fighting alongside you."

"Yes," he said. His nostrils flared as he drew in an unhappy breath. "The rest of you. That's what I won't be able to stand. It's too deep in me. I might be able to stand there and let myself be killed. But can I stand there when they start to kill someone else—like Amanda, and she already wounded?"

There was nothing I could say to him. But the irony of it rang in me, just the same. Both he and Amanda, afraid that their instincts would lead them to do what their thinking minds had told them they should not do. He and I walked back to his office in silence. When we arrived, there was a message that had been left with Michael's orderly, for me, to call Ian.

I did. His face looked out of the phone screen at me, as unchanged as ever.

"The Naharese still haven't started to move," he said. "They're so unprofessional I'm beginning to think that perhaps we can get Padma, at least, away from here. He can take one of the small units from the vehicle pool and fly out toward Nahar City. My guess is that once they stop him and see he's an Exotic, they'll simply wave him on."

"It could be," I said.

"I'd like you to go and put that point to him," said Ian. "He seems to want to stay, for reasons of his own, but he may listen if you make him see that by staying here, he simply increases the load of responsibility on the rest of us. I'd like to order him out of here; but he knows I don't have the authority for that."

"What makes you think I'm the one to talk him into going?"

"It'd have to be one of the senior officers here, to get him to listen," said Ian. "Both Kensie and I are too tied up to take the time. While even if either one was capable, Michael's a bad choice and Amanda's flat in bed."

"All right," I said. "I'll go talk to him right now. Where is he?"

"In his quarters, I understand. Michael can tell you how to find them."

I reached Padma's suite without trouble. In fact, it was not far from the suite of rooms that had been assigned to me. I found Padma seated at his desk making a recording. He broke off when I stepped into his sitting room in answer to his invitation, which had followed my knock on his door.

"If you're busy, I can drop back in a little while," I said.

"No, no," He swung his chair around, away from the desk. "Sit down. I'm just doing up a report for whoever comes out from the Exotics to replace me."

"You won't need to be replaced if you'll leave now," I said. It was a blunt beginning, but he had given me the opening and time was not plentiful.

"I see," he said. "Did Ian or Kensie ask you to talk to me, or is this the result of an impulse of your own?"

"Ian asked me," I said. "The Naharese are delaying their attack, and he thinks that they're so generally disorganized and unmilitary that there's a chance for you to get safely away to Nahar City. They'll undoubtedly stop whatever vehicle you'd take, when they see it coming out of Gebel Nahar. But once they see you're an Exotic—"

His smile interrupted me.

"All right," I said. "Tell me. Why shouldn't they let you pass when they see you're an Exotic? All the worlds know Exotics are noncombatants."

"Perhaps," he said. "Unfortunately, William has made a practice of identifying us as the machiavellian practitioners at the roots of whatever trouble and evil there is to be found anywhere. At the moment most of the Naharese have an image of me that's half-demon, half-enemy. In their present mood of license, most of them would probably welcome the chance to shoot me on sight."

I stared at him. He was smiling.

"If that's the case, why didn't you leave days ago?" I asked him.

"I have my duty, too. In this instance, it's to gather information for those on Mara and Kultis." His smile broadened. "Also, there's the matter of my own temperament. Watching a situation like the one here is fascinating. I wouldn't leave now if I could. In short, I'm as chained here as the rest of you, even if it is for different reasons."

I shook my head at him.

"It's a fine argument," I said. "But if you'll forgive me, it's a little hard to believe."

"In what way?"

"I'm sorry," I told him, "but I don't seem to be able to give any real faith to the idea that you're being held here by patterns that are essentially the same as mine, for instance."

"Not the same," he said. "Equivalent. The fact others can't match you Dorsai in your own particular area doesn't mean those others don't have equal areas in which equal commitments apply to them. The physics of life works in all of us. It simply manifests itself differently with different people."

"With identical results?"

"With comparable results—could I ask you to sit down?" Padma said mildly. "I'm getting a stiff neck looking up at you."

I sat down facing him.

"For example," he said. "In the Dorsai ethic, you and the others here have something that directly justifies your natural human hunger to do things for great purposes. The Naharese here have no equivalent ethic; but they feel the hunger just the same. So they invent their own customs, their *leto de muerte* concepts. But can you Dorsais, of all people, deny that their concepts can lead them to as true a heroism, or as true a keeping of faith as your ethic leads you to?"

"Of course I can't deny," I said. "But my people can at least be counted on to perform as expected. Can the Naharese?"

"No. But note the dangers of the fact that Dorsais are known to be trustworthy, Exotics known to be per-

sonally nonviolent, the church soldiers of the Friendly Worlds known to be faith-holders. That very knowledge tends too often to lead one to take for granted that trustworthiness is the exclusive property of the Dorsai, that there are no truly non-violent individuals not wearing Exotic robes, and that the faith of anyone not a Friendly must be weak and unremarkable. We are all human and struck with the whole spectrum of the human nature. For clear thinking, it's necessary to first assume that the great hungers and responses are there in everyone—then simply go look for them in all people—including the Naharese."

"You sound a little like Michael when you get on the subject of the Naharese." I got up. "All right, have it your way and stay if you want. I'm going to leave now, myself, before you talk me into going out and offering to surrender before they even get here."

He laughed. I left.

It was time again for me to check Amanda. I went to the medical section. But she was honestly asleep now. Apparently she had been able to put her personal concerns aside enough so that she could exercise a little of the basic physiological control we are all taught from birth. If she had, it could be that she would spend most of the next twenty-four hours sleeping, which would be the best thing for her. If the Naharese did not manage, before that time was up, to break through to the inner fort where the medical section was, she would have taken a large stride toward healing herself. If they did break through she would need whatever strength she could gain between now and then.

It was a shock to see the sun as high in the sky as it was, when I emerged from the blind walls of the corridors once more, on to the first terrace. The sky was almost perfectly clear and there was a small, steady breeze. The day would be hot. Ian and Kensie were each standing at one end of the terrace and looking through watch cameras at the Naharese front.

Michael, the only other person in sight, was also at a watch camera, directly in front of the door I had come out. I went to him and he looked up as I reached him.

"They're on the move," he said, stepping back from the watch camera. I looked into its rectangular viewing screen, bright with the daylight scene it showed under the shadow of the battle armor hooding the camera. He was right. The regiments had finally formed for the attack and were now moving toward us with their portable field weapons, at the pace of a slow walk across the intervening plain.

I could see their regimental and company flags spaced out along the front of the crescent formation and whipping in the morning breeze. The Guard Regiment was still in the center and Michael's Third Regiment out on the right wing. Behind the two wings I could see the darker swarms that were the volunteers and the revolutionaries, in their civilian clothing.

The attacking force had already covered a third of the distance to us. I stepped away from the screen of the camera, and all at once the front of men I looked at became a thin line with little bright flashes of reflected sunlight and touches of color all along it, still distant under the near-cloudless sky and the climbing sun.

"Another thirty or forty minutes before they reach us," said Michael.

I looked at him. The clear daylight showed him as pale and wire-tense. He looked as if he had been whittled down until nothing but nerves were left. He was not wearing weapons, although at either end of the terrace, Ian and Kensie both had sidearms clipped to their legs, and behind us there were racks of cone rifles ready for use.

The rifles woke me to something I had subconsciously noted but not focused upon. The bays with the fixed weapons were empty of human figures.

"Where're your bandsmen?" I asked Michael.

He gazed at me.

"They're gone," he said.

"Gone?"

"Decamped. Run off. Deserted, if you want to use that word."

I stared at him.

"You mean they've joined—"

"No, no." He broke in on me as if the question I was just about to ask was physically painful to him. "They haven't gone over to the enemy. They just decided to save their own skins. I told you—you remember, I told you they might. You can't blame them. They're not Dorsai; and staying here meant certain death for them."

"If Gebel Nahar is overrun," I said.

"Can you believe it won't be?"

"It's become hard to," I said, "now that there's just us. But there's always a chance as long as anyone's left to fight. At Baunpore, I saw men and women firing from hospital beds, when the North Freilanders broke in."

I should not have said it. I saw the shadow cross his

eyes and knew he had taken my reference to Baunpore personally, as if I had been comparing his present weaponless state with the last efforts of the defenders I had seen then. There were times when my scars became more curse than blessing.

"That's a general observation, only," I told him. "I don't mean to accuse—"

"It's not what you accuse me of, it's what I accuse

me of," he said, in a low voice looking out at the on-coming regiments. "I knew what it meant when my bandsmen took off. But I also understand how they could decide to do it."

There was nothing more I could say. We both knew that without his forty men we could not even make a pretence of holding the first terrace past the moment when the first line of Naharese would reach the base of the ramparts. There were just too few of us and too many of them to stop them from coming over the top.

"They're probably hiding just out beyond the walls," he said. He was still talking about his former bandsmen. "If we do manage to hold out for a day or two, there's a slight chance they might trickle back—"

He broke off, staring past me. I turned and saw Amanda.

How she had managed to do it by herself, I do not know. But, clearly, she had gotten herself out of her hospital bed and strapped the portable drainage unit on to her. It was not heavy or much bigger than a thick book; and it was designed for wearing by an am-bulatory patient, but it must have been hell for her to rig it by herself with that tube rubbing inside her at every deep breath.

Now she was here, looking as if she might collapse at any time, but on her feet with the unit slung from her right shoulder and strapped to her right side. She had a sidearm clipped to her left thigh, over the cloth of the hospital gown; and the gown itself had been ripped up the center so that she could walk in it.

"What the hell are you doing up here?" I snarled at her. "Get back to bed!"

"Corunna—" she gave me the most level and un-yielding stare I have ever encountered from anyone in my life, "don't give me orders. I rank you."

I blinked at her. It was true I had been asked to be her driver for the trip here, and in a sense that put me under her orders. But for her to presume to tell a Captain of a full flight of fighting ships, with an edge of half a dozen years in seniority and experience that in a combat situation like this she ranked him—it was raving nonsense. I opened my mouth to explode—and found myself bursting out in laughter, instead. The situation was too ridiculous. Here we were, five people even counting Michael, facing three thousand; and I was about to let myself get trapped into an argument over who ranked who. Aside from the fact that only the accident of her present assignment gave her any claim to superiority over me, relative rank between Dorsai had always been a matter of local conditions and situations, tempered with a large pinch of common sense.

But, obviously she was out here on the terrace to stay; and obviously, I was not going to make any real issue of it under the circumstances. We both understood what was going on. Which did not change the fact that she should not have been on her feet. Like Ian out on the plain, and in spite of having been forced to see the funny side of it, I was still angry with her.

"The next time you're wounded, you better hope I'm not your medico," I told her. "What do you think you can do up here, anyway?"

"I can be with the rest of you," she said.

I closed my mouth again. There was no arguing with that answer. Out of the corner of my eyes I saw Kensie and Ian approaching from the far ends of the

terrace. In a moment they were with us.

They looked down at her but said nothing, and we all turned to look again out across the plain.

The Naharese front had been approaching steadily. It was still too far away to be seen as a formation of individuals. It was still just a line of different shade than the plain itself, touched with flashes of light and spots of color. But it was a line with a perceptible thickness now.

We stood together, the four of us, looking at the slow, ponderous advance upon us. All my life, as just now with Amanda, I had been plagued by a sudden awareness of the ridiculous. It came on me now. What mad god had decided that an army should march against a handful—and that the handful should not only stand to be marched upon, but should prepare to fight back? But then the sense of the ridiculousness passed. The Naharese would continue to come on because all their lives had oriented them against Gebel Nahar. We would oppose them when they came because all our lives had been oriented to fighting for even lost causes, once we had become committed to them. In another time and place it might be different for those of us on both sides. But this was the here and now.

With that, I passed into the final stage that always came on me before battle. It was as if I stepped down into a place of private peace and quiet. What was coming would come, and I would meet it when it came. I was aware of Kensie, Ian, Michael and Amanda standing around me, and aware that they were experiencing much the same feelings. Something like a telepathy flowed between us, binding us together in a feeling of particular unity. In my life there has been nothing like that feeling of unity, and I have noticed that those who have once felt it never forget it. It is as it is, as it always has been, and we who are there at that moment are together. Against that togetherness, odds no longer matter.

There was a faint scuff of a foot on the terrace floor, and Michael was gone. I looked at the others, and the thought was unspoken between us. He had gone to put on his weapons. We turned once more to the plain, and saw the approaching Naharese now close enough so that they were recognizable as individual figures. They were almost close enough for the sound of their approach to be heard by us.

We moved forward to the parapet of the terraces and stood watching. The day-breeze, strengthening, blew in our faces. There was time now to appreciate the sunlight, the not-yet-hot temperature of the day and the moving air. Another few hundred meters and they would be within the range of maximum efficiency for our emplaced weapons—and we, of course, within range of their portables. Until then, there was nothing urgent to be done.

The door opened behind us. I turned, but it was not Michael. It was Padma, supporting El Conde, who was coming out to us with the help of a silver-headed walking stick. Padma helped him out to where we stood at the parapet, and for a second he ignored us, looking instead out at the oncoming troops. Then he turned to us.

"Gentlemen and lady," he said in Spanish, "I have chosen to join you."

"We're honored," Ian answered him in the same

tongue. "Would you care to sit down?"

"Thank you, no. I will stand. You may go about your duties."

He leaned on the cane, watching across the parapet and paying no attention to us. We stepped back away from him, and Padma spoke in a low voice.

"I'm sure he won't be in the way," Padma said. "But he wanted to be down here, and there was no one but me left to help him."

"It's all right," said Kensie. "But what about you?"

"I'd like to stay, too," said Padma.

Ian nodded. A harsh sound came from the throat of the count, and we looked at him. He was rigid as some ancient dry spearshaft, staring out at the approaching soldiers, his face carved with the lines of fury and scorn.

"What is it?" Amanda asked.

I had been as baffled as the rest. Then a faint sound came to my ear. The regiments were at last close enough to be heard; and what we were hearing were their regimental bands—except Michael's band, of course—as a faint snatch of melody on the breeze. It was barely hearable, but I recognized it, as El Conde obviously already had.

"They're playing the *te guelo*," I said. "Announcing *'no quarter.'*"

The *te guelo* is a promise to cut the throat of anyone opposing. Amanda's eyebrows rose.

"For us?" she said. "What good do they think that's going to do?"

"They may think Michael's bandsmen are still with us, and perhaps they're hoping to scare them out," I said. "But probably they're doing it just because it's always done when they attack."

The others listened for a second. The *te guelo* is an effectively chilling piece of music; but, as Amanda had implied, it was a little beside the point to play it to Dorsai who had already made their decision to fight.

"Where's Michael?" she asked now.

I looked around. It was a good question. If he had indeed gone for weapons, he should have been back out on the terrace by this time. But there was no sign of him.

"I don't know," I said.

"They've stopped their portable weapons," Kensie said, "and they're setting them up to fire. Still out of effective range, against walls like this."

"We'd probably be better down behind the armor of our own embayments and ready to fire back when they

get a little closer," said Ian. "They can't hurt the walls from where they are. They might get lucky and hurt some of us."

He turned to El Conde.

"If you'd care to step down into one of the weapon embayments, sir—" he said.

El Conde shook his head.

"I shall watch from here," he announced.

Ian nodded. He looked at Padma.

"Of course," said Padma. "I'll come in with one of you—unless I can be useful in some other way?"

"No," said Ian. A shouting from the approaching soldiers that drowned out the band music turned him and the rest of us once more toward the plain.

The front line of the attackers had broken into a run toward us. They were only a hundred meters or so now from the foot of the slope leading to the walls of Gebel Nahar. Whether it had been decided that they should attack from that distance, or—more likely—someone had been carried away and started forward early, did not matter. The attack had begun.

For a moment, all of us who knew combat recognized immediately, this development had given us a temporary respite from the portable weapons. With their own soldiers flooding out ahead, it would be difficult for the gunners to fire at Gebel Nahar without killing their own men. It was the sort of small happenstance that can sometimes be turned to an advantage—but, as I stared out at the plain, I had no idea of what we might do that in that moment that would make any real difference to the battle's outcome.

"Look!"

It was Amanda calling. The shouting of the attacking soldiers had stopped, suddenly. She was standing right at the parapet, pointing out and down. I took one step forward, so that I could see the slope below close by the foot of the first wall, and saw what she had seen.

The front line of the attackers was full of men trying to slow down against the continued pressure of those behind who had not yet seen what those in front had. The result was effectively a halting of the attack as more and more of them stared at what was happening on the slope.

What was happening there was that the lid of El Conde's private exit from Gebel Nahar was rising. To the Naharese military it must have looked as if some secret weapon was about to unveil itself on the slope— and it would have been this that had caused them to have sudden doubts and their front line of men to dig in their heels. They were still a good two or three hundred meters from the tunnel entrance, and the first line of attackers, trapped where they were by those behind them, must have suddenly conceived of themselves as sitting ducks for whatever field-class weapon would elevate itself through this unexpected opening and zero in on them.

But of course no such weapon came out. Instead, what emerged was what looked like a head wearing a regimental cap, with a stick tilted back by its right ear . ... and slowly, up on to the level of the ground, and out to face them all came Michael.

He was still without weapons. But he was now dressed in his full parade regimentals as band officer; and the *gaita gallega* was resting in his arms and on his shoulder, the mouthpiece between his lips, the long drone over his shoulder. He stepped out on to the slope of the hill and began to march down it, toward the Naharese.

The silence was deadly; and into that silence, striking up, came the sound of the *gaita gallega* as he started to play it. Clear and strong it came to us on the wall; and clearly it reached as well to the now-silent and motionless ranks of the Naharese. He was playing *Su Madre*.

He went forward at a march step, shoulders level, the instrument held securely in his arms; and his playing went before him, throwing its challenge directly into their faces. A single figure marching against six thousand.

From where I stood, I had a slight angle on him; and with the help of the magnification of the screen on the watch camera next to me, I could get just a glimpse of his face from the side and behind him. He looked peaceful and intent. The exhausted leanness and tension I had seen in him earlier seemed to have gone out of him. He marched as if on parade, with the intentness of a good musician in performance, and all the time *Su Madre* was hooting and mocking at the armed regiments before him.

I touched the controls of the camera to make it give me a closeup look at the men in the front of the Naharese force. They stood as if paralyzed, as I panned along their line. They were saying nothing, doing nothing, only watching Michael come toward them as if he meant to march right through them. All along their front, they were stopped and watching.

But their inaction was something that could not last —a moment of shock that had to wear off. Even as I watched, they began to stir and speak. Michael was

between us and them, and with the incredible voice of the bagpipe his notes came almost loudly to our ears. But rising behind them, we now began to hear a low-pitched swell of sound like the growl of some enormous beast.

I looked in the screen. The regiments were still not advancing, but none of the figures I now saw as I panned down the front were standing frozen with shock. In the middle of the crescent formation, the soldiers of the Guard Regiment who held a feud with Michael's own Third Regiment, were shaking weapons and fists at him and shouting. I had no way of knowing what they were saying, at this distance, and the camera could not help me with that, but I had no doubt that they were answering challenge with challenge, insult with insult.

All along the line, the front boiled, becoming more active every minute. They had all seen that Michael was unarmed; and for a few moments this held them in check. They threatened, but did not offer to, fire on him. But even at this distance I could feel the fury building up in them. It was only a matter of time, I thought, until one of them lost his self-control and used the weapon he carried.

I wanted to shout at Michael to turn around and come back to the tunnel. He had broken the momentum of their attack and thrown them into confusion. With troops like this they would certainly not take up their advance where they had halted it. It was almost a certainty that after this challenge, this emotional shock, that their senior officers would pull them back and reform them before coming on again. A valuable breathing space had been gained. It could be some hours, it could be not until tomorrow they would be able to mount a second attack; and in that time internal tensions or any number of developments might work to help us further. Michael still had them between his thumb and forefinger. If he turned his back on them now, their inaction might well hold until he was back in safety.

But there was no way I could reach him with that message. And he showed no intention of turning back on his own. Instead he went steadily forward, scorning them with his music, taunting them for attacking in their numbers an opponent so much less than themselves.

Still the Naharese soldiery only shook their weapons

and shouted insults at him; but now in the screen I began to see a difference. On the wing occupied by the Third Regiment there were uniformed figures beginning to wave Michael back. I moved the view of the screen further out along that wing and saw individuals in civilian clothes, some of those from the following swarm of volunteers and revolutionaries, who were pushing their way to the front, kneeling down and putting weapons to their shoulders.

The Third Regiment soldiers were pushing these others back and jerking their weapons away from them. Fights were beginning to break out; but on that wing, those who wished to fire on Michael were being held back. It was plain that the Third Regiment was torn now between its commitment to join in the attack on Gebel Nahar and its impulse to protect their former bandmaster in his act of outrageous bravery. Still, I saw one civilian with the starved face of a fanatic who had literally to be tackled and held on the ground by three of the Third Regiment before he could be stopped from firing on Michael.

A sudden cold suspicion passed through me. I swung the view of the screen to the opposite wing; and there I saw the same situation. From behind the uniformed soldiers there, volunteers and civilian revolutionaries were trying to stop Michael with their weapons. Some undoubtedly were from the neighboring principalities where a worship of drama and acts of flamboyant courage was not part of the culture, as it was here. On this wing, also, the soldiers were trying to stop those individuals who attempted to shoot Michael. But here, the effort to prevent that firing was scattered and ineffective.

I saw a number of weapons of all types leveled at Michael. No sound could reach me, and only the sport guns and ancient explosive weapons showed any visible sign that they were being fired; but it was clear that death was finally in the air around Michael.

I switched the view hastily back to him. For a moment he continued to march forward in the screen as if some invisible armor was protecting him. Then he stumbled slightly, caught himself, went forward, and fell.

For a second time—for a moment only—the voice of the attackers stopped, cut off as if a multitude of invisible hands had been clapped over the mouths of those there. I lifted the view on the screen from the fallen shape of Michael and saw soldiers and civilians alike standing motionless, staring at him, as if they could not believe that he had at last been brought down.

Then, on the wing opposite to that held by the Third Regiment, the civilians that had been firing began to dance and wave their weapons in the air— and suddenly the whole formation seemed to collapse inward, the two wings melting back into the main body as the soldiers of the Third Regiment charged across the front to get at the rejoicing civilians, and the Guard Regiment swirled out to oppose them. The fighting spread as individual attacked individual. In a moment they were all embroiled. A wild mob without direction or purpose of any kind, except to kill whoever was closest, took the place of the military formation that had existed only five minutes before.

As the fighting became general, the tight mass of bodies spread out like butter rapidly melting down from a solid to a liquid; and the struggle spread out over a larger and larger area, until at last it covered even the place where Michael had fallen. Amanda turned away from the parapet and I caught her as she staggered. I held her upright and she leaned heavily against me.

"I have to lie down, I guess," she murmured.

I led her towards the door and the bed that was waiting for her back in the medical section. Ian, Kensie and Padma turned and followed, leaving only El Conde, leaning on his silver-headed stick and staring out at what was taking place on the plain, his face lighted with the fierce satisfaction of a hawk perched above the body of its kill.

It was twilight before all the fighting had ceased; and, with the dark, there began to be heard the small sounds of the annunciator chimes at the main gate. One by one Michael's bandsmen began to slip back to us in Gebel Nahar. With their return, Ian, Kensie and I were able to stop taking turns at standing watch, as we had up until then. But it was not until after midnight that we felt it was safe to leave long enough to go out and recover Michael's body.

Amanda insisted on going with us. There was no reason to argue against her coming with us and a good deal of reason in favor of it. She was responding very well to the drainage unit and a further eight hours of sleep had rebuilt her strength to a remarkable degree. Also, she was the one who suggested we take Michael's body back to the Dorsai for burial.

The cost of travel between the worlds was such that few individuals could afford it; and few Dorsai who died in the course of their duties off-planet had their

bodies returned for internment in native soil. But we had adequate space to carry Michael's body with us in the courier vessel; and it was Amanda's point that Michael had solved the problem by his action—something for which the Dorsai world in general owed him a debt. Both Padma and El Conde had agreed, after what had happened today, that the Naharese would not be brought back to the idea of revolution again for some time. William's machinations had fallen through. Ian and Kensie could now either make it their choice to stay and execute their contract, or legitimately withdraw from it for the reason that they had been faced with situations beyond their control.

In the end, all of us except Padma went out to look for Michael's body, leaving the returned bandsmen to stand duty. It was full night by the time we emerged once more on to the plain through the secret exit.

"El Conde will have to have another of these made for him," commented Kensie, as we came out under the star-brilliant sky. "This passage is more a national monument than a secret, now."

The night was one very much like the one before, when Kensie and I had made our sweep in search of observers from the other side. But this time we were looking only for the dead; and that was all we found.

During the afternoon all the merely wounded had been taken away by their friends; but there were bodies to be seen as we moved out to the spot where we had seen Michael go down, but not many of them. It had been possible to mark the location exactly using the surveying equipment built into the watch cameras. But the bodies were not many. The fighting had been more a weaponed brawl than a battle. Which did not alter the fact that those who had died were dead. They would not come to life again, any more than Michael would. A small night breeze touched our faces from time to time as we walked. It was too soon after the fighting for the odors of death to have taken possession of the battlefield. For the present moment under the stars the scene we saw, including the dead bodies, had all the neatness and antiseptic quality of a stage setting.

We came to the place where Michael's body should have been, but it was gone. Ian switched on a pocket lamp; and he, with Kensie, squatted to examine the ground. I waited with Amanda. Ian and Kensie were

the experienced field officers, with Hunter Team practise. I could spend several hours looking, to see what they would take in at a glance.

After a few minutes they stood up again and Ian switched off the lamp. There were a few seconds while our eyes readjusted, and then the plain became real around us once more, replacing the black wall of darkness that the lamplight had instantly created.

"He was here, all right," Kensie said. "Evidently quite a crowd came to carry his body off someplace else. It'll be easy enough to follow the way they went."

We followed the trail of scuffed earth and broken vegetation left by the footwear of those who had carried away Michael's body. The track they had left was plain enough so that I myself had no trouble picking it out, even by starlight, as we went along at a walk. It led further away from Gebel Nahar, toward where the center of the Naharese formation had been when the general fighting broke out; and as we went, bodies became more numerous. Eventually, at a spot which must have been close to where the Guard Regiment had stood, we found Michael.

The mound on which his body lay was visible as a dark mass in the starlight, well before we reached it. But it was only when Ian switched on his pocket lamp again that we saw its true identity and purpose. It was a pile nearly a meter in height and a good two meters long and broad. Most of what made it up was clothes; but there were many others things mixed in with the cloth items—belts and ornamental chains, ancient weapons, so old that they must have been heirlooms, bits of personal jewelry, even shoes and boots. But, as I say, the greater part of what made it up was clothing—in particular uniform jackets or shirts, although a fair number of detached sleeves or collars bearing insignia of rank had evidently been deliberately torn off by their owners and added as separate items.

On top of all this, lying on his back with his dead face turned toward the stars, was Michael. I did not need an interpretation of what I was seeing here, after my earlier look at the painting in the Nahar City Spaceport Terminal. Michael lay not with a sword, but with the *gaita gallega* held to his chest; and beneath him was the *leto de muerte*—the real *leto de muerte*, made up of everything that those who had seen him there that day, and who had fought for and against him after it was too late, considered the most valuable thing they could give from what was in their possession at the time.

Each had given the best he could, to build up a bed of state for the dead hero—a bed of triumph, actually, for in winning here Michael had won everything, according to their rules and their ways. After the supreme victory of his courage, as they saw it, there was nothing left for them but the offering of tribute; their possessions or their lives.

We stood, we three, looking at it all in silence. Finally, Kensie spoke.

"Do you still want to take him home?"

"No," said Amanda. The word was almost as a sigh from her, as she stood looking at the dead Michael. "No. This is his home, now."

We went back to Gebel Nahar, leaving the corpse of Michael with its honor guard of the other dead around him.

The next day Amanda and I left Gebel Nahar to return to the Dorsai. Kensie and Ian had decided to complete their contract; and it looked as if they should be able to do so without difficulty. With dawn, individual soldiers of the regiments had begun pouring back into Gebel Nahar, asking to be accepted once more into their duties. They were eager to please, and for Naharese, remarkably subdued.

Padma was also leaving. He rode into the spaceport with us, as did Kensie and Ian, who had come along to see us off. In the terminal, we stopped to look once more at the *leto de muerte* painting.

"Now I understand," said Amanda, after a moment. She turned from the painting and lightly touched both Ian and Kensie who were standing on either side of her.

"We'll be back," she said, and led the two of them off.

I was left with Padma.

"Understand?" I said to him. "The *leto de muerte* concept?"

"No," said Padma, softly. "I think she meant that now she understands what Michael came to understand, and how it applies to her. How it applies to everyone, including me and you."

I felt coldness on the back of my neck.

"To me?" I said.

"You have lost part of your protection, the armor of your sorrow and loss," he answered. "To a certain extent, when you let yourself become concerned with Michael's problem, you let someone else in to touch you again."

I looked at him, a little grimly.

"You think so?" I put the matter aside. "I've got to get out and start the checkover on the ship. Why don't you come along? When Amanda and the others come back and don't find us here, they'll know where to look."

Padma shook his head.

"I'm afraid I'd better say goodby now," he replied. "There are other urgencies that have been demanding my attention for some time and I've put them aside for this. Now, it's time to pay them some attention. So I'll say goodby now; and you can give my farewells to the others."

"Goodby, then," I said.

As when we had met, he did not offer me his hand; but the warmth of him struck through to me; and for the first time I faced the possibility that perhaps he was right. That Michael, or he, or Amanda—or perhaps the whole affair—had either worn thin a spot, or chipped off a piece, of that shell that had closed around me when I watched them kill Else.

"Perhaps we'll run into each other again," I said.

"With people like ourselves," he said, "it's very likely."

He smiled once more, turned and went.

I crossed the terminal to the Security Section, identified myself and went out to the courier ship. It was no more than half an hour's work to run the checkover— these special vessels are practically self-monitoring. When I finished the others had still not yet appeared. I was about to go in search of them when Amanda pulled herself through the open entrance port and closed it behind her.

"Where's Kensie and Ian?" I asked.

"They were paged. The Board of Governors showed up at Gebel Nahar, without warning. They both had to hurry back for a full-dress confrontation. I told them I'd say goodby to you for them."

"All right. Padma sends his farewells by me to the rest of you."

She laughed and sat down in the copilot's seat beside me.

"I'll have to write Ian and Kensie to pass Padma's on," she said. "Are we ready to lift?"

"As soon as we're cleared for it. That port sealed?"

She nodded. I reached out to the instrument bank before me, keyed Traffic Control and asked to be put in sequence for liftoff. Then I gave my attention to the matter of warming the bird to life.

Thirty-five minutes later we lifted, and another ten minutes after that saw us safely clear of the atmosphere. I headed out for the legally requisite number of planetary diameters before making the first phase shift. Then, finally, with mind and hands free, I was able to turn my attention again to Amanda.

She was lost in thought, gazing deep into the pinpoint fires of the visible stars in the navigation screen above the instrument bank. I watched her without speaking for a moment, thinking again that Padma had possibly been right. Earlier, even when she had spoken to me in the dark of my room of how she felt about Ian, I had touched nothing of her. But now, I could feel the life in her as she sat beside me.

She must have sensed my eyes on her, because she roused from her private consultation with the stars and looked over.

"Something on your mind?" she asked.

"No," I said. "Or rather, yes. I didn't really follow your thinking, back in the terminal when we were looking at the painting and you said that now you understood."

"You didn't?" She watched me for a fraction of a second. "I meant that now I understood what Michael had."

"Padma said he thought you'd meant you understood how it applied to you—and to everyone."

She did not answer for a second.

"You're wondering about me—and Ian and Kensie," she said.

"It's not important what I wonder," I said.

"Yes, it is. After all, I dumped the whole matter in your lap in the first place, without warning. It's going to be all right. They'll finish up their contract here and then Ian will go to Earth for Leah. They'll be married and she'll settle in Foralie."

"And Kensie?"

"Kensie." She smiled sadly. "Kensie'll go on . . . his own way."

"And you?"

"I'll go mine." She looked at me very much as Padma had looked at me, as we stood below the painting. "That's what I meant when I said I'd understood. In the end the only way is to be what you are and do what you must. If you do that, everything works. Michael found that out."

"And threw his life away putting it into practise."

"No," she said swiftly. "He threw nothing away. There were only two things he wanted. One was to be the Dorsai he was born to be and the other was never to use a weapon; and it seemed he could have either

207

one but not the other. Only, he was true to both and it worked. In the end, he was Dorsai and unarmed— and by being both he stopped an army."

Her eyes held me so powerfully that I could not look away.

"He went his way and found his life," she said, "and my answer is to go mine. Ian, his. And Kensie, his—"

She broke off so abruptly I knew what she had been about to say.

"Give me time," I said; and the words came a little more thickly than I had expected. "It's too soon yet. Still too soon since she died. But give me time, and maybe . . . maybe, even me."

WARRIOR

The spaceliner coming in from New Earth and Freiland, worlds under the Sirian sun, was delayed in its landing by traffic at the spaceport in Long Island Sound. The two police lieutenants, waiting on the bare concrete beyond the shelter of the Terminal buildings, turned up the collars of their cloaks against the hissing sleet, in this unweatherproofed area. The sleet was turning into tiny hailstones that bit and stung all exposed areas of skin. The gray November sky poured them down without pause or mercy; the vast, reaching surface of concrete seemed to dance with their white multitudes.

"Here it comes now," said Tyburn, the Manhattan Complex police lieutenant, risking a glance up into the hailstorm. "Let me do the talking when we take him in."

"Fine by me," answered Breagan, the spaceport officer, "I'm only here to introduce you—and because it's my bailiwick. You can have Kenebuck, with his hood connections, and his millions. If it were up to me, I'd let the soldier get him."

"It's him," said Tyburn, "who's likely to get the soldier—and that's why I'm here. You ought to know that."

The great mass of the interstellar ship settled like a cautious mountain to the concrete two hundred yards off. It protruded a landing stair near its base like a metal leg, and the passengers began to disembark. The two policemen spotted their man immediately in the crowd.

"He's big," said Breagan, with the judicious appraisal of someone safely on the sidelines, as the two of them moved forward.

"They're all big, these professional military men off the Dorsai world," answered Tyburn, a little irritably, shrugging his shoulders against the cold, under his cloak. "They breed themselves that way."

"I know they're big," said Breagan. "This one's bigger."

The first wave of passengers was rolling toward them now, their quarry among the mass. Tyburn and Breagan moved forward to meet him. When they got close they could see, even through the hissing sleet, every line of his dark, unchanging face looming above the lesser heights of the people around him, his military erectness molding the civilian clothes he wore until they might as well have been a uniform. Tyburn found himself staring fixedly at the tall figure as it came toward him. He had met such professional soldiers from the Dorsai before, and the stamp of their breeding had always been plain on them. But this man was somehow more so, even than the others Tyburn had seen. In some way he seemed to be the spirit of the Dorsai, incarnate.

He was one of twin brothers, Tyburn remembered now from the dossier back at his office. Ian and Kensie were their names, of the Graeme family at Foralie, on the Dorsai. And the report was that Kensie had two men's likability, while his brother Ian, now approaching Tyburn, had a double portion of grim shadow and solitary darkness.

Staring at the man coming toward him, Tyburn could believe the dossier now. For a moment, even, with the sleet and the cold taking possession of him, he found himself believing in the old saying that, if the born soldiers of the Dorsai ever cared to pull back to their own small, rocky world, and challenge the rest of humanity, not all the thirteen other inhabited planets could stand against them. Once, Tyburn had laughed at that idea. Now, watching Ian approach, he could not laugh. A man like this would live for different reasons from those of ordinary men—and die for different reasons.

Tyburn shook off the wild notion. The figure coming toward him, he reminded himself sharply, was a professional military man—nothing more.

Ian was almost to them now. The two policemen moved in through the crowd and intercepted him.

"Commandant Ian Graeme?" said Breagan. "I'm Kaj Breagan of the spaceport police. This is Lieutenant Walter Tyburn of the Manhattan Complex Force. I wonder if you could give us a few minutes of your time?"

Ian Graeme nodded, almost indifferently. He turned and paced along with them, his longer stride making more leisurely work of their brisk walking, as they led him away from the route of the disembarking passengers and in through a blank metal door at one end of the Terminal, marked *Unauthorized Entry Prohibited*. Inside, they took an elevator tube up to the offices on the Terminal's top floor, and ended up in chairs around a desk in one of the offices.

All the way in, Ian had said nothing. He sat in his chair now with the same indifferent patience, gazing at Tyburn, behind the desk, and at Breagan, seated back against the wall at the desk's right side. Tyburn found himself staring back in fascination. Not at the granite face, but at the massive, powerful hands of the man, hanging idly between the chair-arms that supported his forearms. Tyburn, with an effort, wrenched his gaze from those hands.

"Well, Commandant," he said, forcing himself at last to look up into the dark, unchanging features, "you're here on Earth for a visit, we understand."

"To see the next-of-kin of an officer of mine." Ian's voice, when he spoke at last, was almost mild compared to the rest of his appearance. It was a deep, calm voice, but lightless—like a voice that had long forgotten the need to be angry or threatening. Only . . . there was something sad about it, Tyburn thought.

"A James Kenebuck?" said Tyburn.

"That's right," answered the deep voice of Ian. "His younger brother, Brian Kenebuck, was on my staff in the recent campaign on Freiland. He died three months back."

"Do you," said Tyburn, "always visit your deceased officers' next of kin?"

"When possible. Usually, of course, they die in the line of duty."

"I see," said Tyburn. The office chair in which he sat seemed hard and uncomfortable underneath him. He shifted slightly. "You don't happen to be armed, do you, Commandant?"

Ian did not even smile.

"No," he said.

"Of course, of course," said Tyburn, uncomfortable. "Not that it makes any difference." He was looking again, in spite of himself, at the two massive, relaxed hands opposite him. "Your . . . extremities by themselves are lethal weapons. We register professional karate and boxing experts here, you know—or did you know?"

Ian nodded.

"Yes," said Tyburn. He wet his lips, and then was furious with himself for doing so. Damn my orders, he thought suddenly and whitely, I don't have to sit here

215

making a fool of myself in front of this man, no matter how many connections and millions Kenebuck owns.

"All right, look here, Commandant," he said, harshly, leaning forward. "We've had a communication from the Freiland-North Police about you. They suggest that you hold Kenebuck—James Kenebuck—responsible for his brother Brian's death."

Ian sat looking back at him without answering.

"Well," demanded Tyburn, raggedly after a long moment, "do you?"

"Force-leader Brian Kenebuck," said Ian calmly, "led his Force, consisting of thirty-six men at the time, against orders, farther than was wise into enemy perimeter. His Force was surrounded and badly shot up. Only he and four men returned to the lines. He was brought to trial in the field under the Mercenaries Code for deliberate mishandling of his troops under combat conditions. The four men who had returned with him testified against him. He was found guilty and I ordered him shot."

Ian stopped speaking. His voice had been perfectly even, but there was so much finality about the way he spoke that after he finished there was a pause in the room while Tyburn and Breagan stared at him as if they had both been tranced. Then the silence, echoing in Tyburn's ears, jolted him back to life.

"I don't see what all this has to do with James Kenebuck, then," said Tyburn. "Brian committed some . . . military crime, and was executed for it. You say you gave the order. If anyone's responsible for Brian Kenebuck's death then, it seems to me it'd be you. Why connect it with someone who wasn't even there at the time, someone who was here on Earth all the while, James Kenebuck?"

"Brian," said Ian, "was his brother."

The emotionless statement was calm and coldly reasonable in the silent, brightly-lit office. Tyburn found his open hands had shrunk themselves into fists on the desk top. He took a deep breath and began to speak in a flat, official tone.

"Commandant," he said, "I don't pretend to understand you. You're a man of the Dorsai, a product of one of the splinter cultures out among the stars. I'm just an old-fashioned Earthborn—but I'm a policeman in the Manhattan Complex and James Kenebuck is . . . well, he's a taxpayer in the Manhattan Complex."

He found he was talking without meeting Ian's eyes. He forced himself to look at them—they were dark unmoving eyes.

"It's my duty to inform you," Tyburn went on, "that we've had intimations to the effect that you're to bring some retribution to James Kenebuck, because of Brian Kenebuck's death. These are only intimations, and as long as you don't break any laws here on Earth, you're free to go where you want and see whom you like. But this *is Earth, Commandant.*"

He paused, hoping that Ian would make some sound, some movement. But Ian only sat there, waiting.

"We don't have any Mercenaries Code here, Commandant," Tyburn went on harshly. "We haven't any feud-right, no *droit-de-main.* But we do have laws. Those laws say that, though a man may be the worst murderer alive, until he's brought to book in our courts, under our process of laws, no one is allowed to harm a hair of his head. Now, I'm not here to argue whether this is the best way or not; just to tell you that that's the way things are." Tyburn stared fixedly into the dark eyes. "Now," he said, bluntly, "I know that if you're determined to try to kill Kenebuck without counting the cost, I can't prevent it."

He paused and waited again. But Ian still said nothing.

"I know," said Tyburn, "that you can walk up to him like any other citizen, and once you're within reach you can try to kill him with your bare hands before anyone can stop you. *I* can't stop you in that case. But what I can do is catch you afterwards, if you succeed, and see you convicted and executed for murder. And you *will* be caught and convicted, there's no doubt about it. You can't kill James Kenebuck the way someone like you would kill a man, and get away with it here on Earth—do you understand that, Commandant?"

"Yes," said Ian.

"All right," said Tyburn, letting out a deep breath. "Then you understand. You're a sane man and a Dorsai professional. From what I've been able to learn about the Dorsai, it's one of your military tenets that part of a man's duty to himself is not to throw his life away in a hopeless cause. And this cause of yours to bring Kenebuck to justice for his brother's death, is hopeless."

He stopped. Ian straightened in a movement preliminary to getting up.

"Wait a second," said Tyburn.

He had come to the hard part of the interview. He had prepared his speech for this moment and rehearsed it over and over again—but now he found himself without faith that it would convince Ian.

"One more word," said Tyburn. "You're a man of camps and battlefields, a man of the military; and you must be used to thinking of yourself as a pretty effective individual. But here, on Earth, those special skills of yours are mostly illegal. And without them you're ineffective and helpless. Kenebuck, on the other hand, is just the opposite. He's got money—millions. And he's got connections, some of them nasty. And he was born and raised here in Manhattan Complex." Tyburn stared emphatically at the tall, dark man, willing him to understand. "Do you follow me? If you, for example, should suddenly turn up dead here, we just might not be able to bring Kenebuck to book for it. Where we absolutely could, and would, bring you to book if the situation were reversed. Think about it."

He sat, still staring at Ian. But Ian's face showed no change, or sign that the message had gotten through to him.

"Thank you," Ian said. "If there's nothing more, I'll be going."

"There's nothing more," said Tyburn, defeated. He watched Ian leave. It was only when Ian was gone, and he turned back to Breagen that he recovered a little of his self-respect. For Breagan's face had paled.

Ian went down through the Terminal and took a cab into Manhattan Complex, to the John Adams Hotel. He registered for a room on the fourteenth floor of the transient section of that hotel and inquired about the location of James Kenebuck's suite in the resident section; then sent his card up to Kenebuck with a request to come by to see the millionaire. After that, he went on up to his own room, unpacked his luggage, which had already been delivered from the spaceport, and took out a small, sealed package. Just at that moment there was a soft chiming sound and his card was returned to him from a delivery slot in the room wall. It fell into the salver below the slot and he picked it up,

to read what was written on the face of it. The penciled
note read:
                    Come on up—
                        K.

He tucked the card and the package into a pocket
and left his transient room. And Tyburn, who had followed him to the hotel, and who had been observing
all of Ian's actions from the second of his arrival,
through sensors placed in the walls and ceilings, half
rose from his chair in the room of the empty suite directly above Kenebuck's, which had been quietly
taken over as a police observation post. Then, help-
lessly, Tyburn swore and sat down again, to follow
Ian's movements in the screen fed by the sensors. So
far there was nothing the policeman could do legally—
nothing but watch.

So he watched as Ian strode down the softly
carpeted hallway to the elevator tube, rose in it to the
eightieth floor and stepped out to face the heavy, transparent door sealing off the resident section of the hotel.
He held up Kenebuck's card with its message to a con-
cierge screen beside the door, and with a soft sigh of air
the door slid back to let him through. He passed on in,
found a second elevator tube, and took it up thirteen
more stories. Black doors opened before him—and he
stepped one step forward into a small foyer to find
himself surrounded by three men.

They were big men—one, a lantern-jawed giant,
was even bigger than Ian—and they were vicious.
Tyburn, watching through the sensor in the foyer ceiling that had been secretly placed there by the police
the day before, recognized all of them from his files.
They were underworld muscle hired by Kenebuck at
word of Ian's coming; all armed, and brutal and hair-
trigger—mad dogs of the lower city. After that first

step into their midst, Ian stood still. And there followed a strange, unnatural cessation of movement in
the room.

The three stood checked. They had been about to
put their hands on Ian to search him for something,
Tyburn saw, and probably to rough him up in the process. But something had stopped them, some abrupt
change in the air around them. Tyburn, watching,
felt the change as they did; but for a moment he felt it
without understanding. Then understanding came to
him.

The difference was in Ian, in the way he stood there.
He was, saw Tyburn, simply . . . waiting. That same
patient indifference Tyburn had seen upon him in the
Terminal office was there again. In the split second of
his single step into the room he had discovered the
men, had measured them, and stopped. Now, he
waited, in his turn, for one of them to make a move.

A sort of black lightning had entered the small foyer.
It was abruptly obvious to the watching Tyburn, as to
the three below, that the first of them to lay hands on
Ian would be the first to find the hands of the Dorsai
soldier upon him—and those hands were death.

For the first time in his life, Tyburn saw the personal power of the Dorsai fighting man, made plain
without words. Ian needed no badge upon him, standing as he stood now, to warn that he was dangerous.
The men about him were mad dogs; but, patently, Ian
was a wolf. There was a difference with the three,
which Tyburn now recognized for the first time. Dogs
—even mad dogs—fight, and the losing dog, if he can,
runs away. But no wolf runs. For a wolf wins every
fight but one, and in that one he dies.

After a moment, when it was clear that none of the

three would move, Ian stepped forward. He passed through them without even brushing against one of them, to the inner door opposite, and opened it and went on through.

He stepped into a three-level living room stretching to a large, wide window, its glass rolled up, and black with the sleet-filled night. The living room was as large as a small suite in itself, and filled with people, men and women, richly dressed. They held cocktail glasses in their hands as they stood or sat, and talked. The atmosphere was heavy with the scents of alcohol, and women's perfumes and cigarette smoke. It seemed that they paid no attention to his entrance, but their eyes followed him covertly once he had passed.

He walked forward through the crowd, picking his way to a figure before the dark window, the figure of a man almost as tall as himself, erect, athletic-looking with a handsome, sharp-cut face under whitish-blond hair that stared at Ian with a sort of incredulity as Ian approached.

"Graeme . . . ?" said this man, as Ian stopped before him. His voice in this moment of off-guard-edness betrayed its two levels, the semi-hoodlum whine and harshness underneath, the polite accents above. "My boys . . . you didn't—" he stumbled, "leave anything with them when you were coming in?"

"No," said Ian. "You're James Kenebuck, of course. You look like your brother." Kenebuck stared at him.

"Just a minute," he said. He set down his glass, turned and went quickly through the crowd and into the foyer, shutting the door behind him. In the hush of the room, those there heard, first silence then a short, unintelligible burst of sharp voices, then silence again.

Kenebuck came back into the room, two spots of angry color high on his cheekbones. He came back to face Ian.

"Yes," he said, halting before Ian. "They were supposed to . . . tell me when you came in." He fell silent, evidently waiting for Ian to speak, but Ian merely stood, examining him, until the spots of color on Kenebuck's cheekbones flared again.

"Well?" he said, abruptly. "Well? You came here to see me about Brian, didn't you? What about Brian?" He added, before Ian could answer, in a tone suddenly brutal: "I know he was shot, so you don't have to break that news to me. I suppose you want to tell me he showed all sorts of noble guts—refused a blindfold and that sort of—"

"No," said Ian. "He didn't die nobly."

Kenebuck's tall, muscled body jerked a little at the words, almost as if the bullets of an invisible firing squad had poured into it.

"Well . . . that's fine!" he laughed angrily. "You come light-years to see me and then you tell me that! I thought you liked him—liked Brian."

"Liked him? No," Ian shook his head. Kenebuck stiffened, his face for a moment caught in a gape of bewilderment. "As a matter of fact," went on Ian, "he was a glory-hunter. That made him a poor soldier and a worse officer. I'd have transferred him out of my command if I'd had time before the campaign on Freiland started. Because of him, we lost the lives of thirty-two men in his Force, that night."

"Oh." Kenebuck pulled himself together, and looked sourly at Ian. "Those thirty-two men. You've got them on your conscience—is that it?"

"No," said Ian. There was no emphasis on the word

as he said it, but somehow to Tyburn's ears above, the brief short negative dismissed Kenebuck's question with an abruptness like contempt. The spots of color on Kenebuck's cheeks flamed.

"You didn't like Brian and your conscience doesn't bother you—what're you here for, then?" he snapped.

"My duty brings me," said Ian.

"Duty?" Kenebuck's face stilled, and went rigid.

Ian reached slowly into his pocket as if he were surrendering a weapon under the guns of an enemy and did not want his move misinterpreted. He brought out the package from his pocket.

"I brought you Brian's personal effects," he said. He turned and laid the package on a table beside Kenebuck. Kenebuck stared down at the package and the color over his cheekbones faded until his face was nearly as pale as his hair. Then slowly, hesitantly, as if he were approaching a booby-trap, he reached out and gingerly picked it up. He held it and turned to Ian, staring into Ian's eyes, almost demandingly.

"It's in here?" said Kenebuck, in a voice barely above a whisper, and with a strange emphasis.

"Brian's effects," said Ian, watching him.

"Yes . . . sure. All right," said Kenebuck. He was plainly trying to pull himself together, but his voice was still almost whispering. "I guess . . . that settles it."

"That settles it," said Ian. Their eyes held together. "Good-by," said Ian. He turned and walked back through the silent crowd and out of the living room. The three muscle-men were no longer in the foyer. He took the elevator tube down and returned to his own hotel room.

Tyburn, who with a key to the service elevators, had

not had to change tubes on the way down as Ian had, was waiting for him when Ian entered. Ian did not seem surprised to see Tyburn there, and only glanced casually at the policeman as he crossed to a decanter of Dorsai whisky that had since been delivered up to the room.

"That's that, then!" burst out Tyburn, in relief. "You got in to see him and he ended up letting you out. You can pack up and go, now. It's over."

"No," said Ian. "Nothing's over yet." He poured a few inches of the pungent, dark whisky into a glass, and moved the decanter over another glass. "Drink?"

"I'm on duty," said Tyburn, sharply.

"There'll be a little wait," said Ian, calmly. He poured some whisky into the other glass, took up both glasses, and stepped across the room to hand one to Tyburn. Tyburn found himself holding it. Ian had stepped on to stand before the wall-high window. Outside, night had fallen; but—faintly seen in the lights from the city levels below—the sleet here above the weather shield still beat like small, dark ghosts against the transparency.

"Hang it, man, what more do you want?" burst out Tyburn. "Can't you see it's you I'm trying to protect —as well as Kenebuck? I don't want *anyone* killed! If you stay around here now, you're asking for it. I keep telling you, here in Manhattan Complex you're the helpless one, not Kenebuck. Do you think he hasn't made plans to take care of you?"

"Not until he's sure," said Ian, turning from the ghost-sleet, beating like lost souls against the window-glass, trying to get in.

"Sure about what? Look, Commandant," said Tyburn, trying to speak calmly, "half an hour after we heard from the Freiland-North Police about you,

Kenebuck called my office to ask for police protection." He broke off, angrily. "Don't look at me like that! How do I know how he found out you were coming? I tell you he's rich, and he's got connections! But the point is, the police protection he's got is just a screen—an excuse—for whatever he's got planned for you on his own. You saw those hoods in the foyer!"

"Yes," said Ian, unemotionally.

"Well, think about it!" Tyburn glared at him. "Look, I don't hold any brief for James Kenebuck! All right—let me tell you about him! We knew he'd been trying to get rid of his brother since Brian was ten—but blast it, Commandant, Brian was no angel, either—"

"I know," said Ian, seating himself in a chair opposite Tyburn.

"All right, you know! I'll tell you anyway!" said Tyburn. "Their grandfather was a local kingpin—he was in every racket on the eastern seaboard. He was one of the mob, with millions he didn't dare count because of where they'd come from. In their father's time, those millions started to be fed into legitimate businesses. The third generation, James and Brian, didn't inherit anything that wasn't legitimate. Hell, we couldn't even make a jaywalking ticket stick against one of them, if we'd ever wanted to. James was twenty and Brian ten when their father died, and when he died the last bit of tattle-tale gray went out of the family linen. But they kept their hoodlum connections, Commandant!"

Ian sat, glass in hand, watching Tyburn almost curiously.

"Don't you get it?" snapped Tyburn. "I tell you that, on paper, in law, Kenebuck's twenty-four carat gilt-edge. But his family was hoodlum, he was raised like a hoodlum, and he thinks like a hood! He didn't want his young brother Brian around to share the crown prince position with him—so he set out to get rid of him. He couldn't just have him killed, so he set out to cut him down, show him up, break his spirit, until Brian took one chance too many trying to match up to his older brother, and killed himself off."

Ian slowly nodded.

"All right!" said Tyburn. "So Kenebuck finally succeeded. He chased Brian until the kid ran off and became a professional soldier—something Kenebuck wouldn't leave his wine, women and song long enough to shine at. And he can shine at most things he really wants to shine at, Commandant. Under that hood attitude and all those millions, he's got a good mind and a good body that he's made a hobby out of training. But, all right. So now it turns out Brian was still no good, and he took some soldiers along when he finally got around to doing what Kenebuck wanted, and getting himself killed. All right! But what can you do about it? What can anyone do about it, with all the connections, and all the money and all the law on Kenebuck's side of it? And, why should you think about doing something about it, anyway?"

"It's my duty," said Ian. He had swallowed half the whisky in his glass, absently, and now he turned the glass thoughtfully around, watching the brown liquor swirl under the forces of momentum and gravity. He looked up at Tyburn. "You know that, Lieutenant."

"Duty! Is duty that important?" demanded Tyburn. Ian gazed at him, then looked away, at the ghost-sleet beating vainly against the glass of the window that held it back in the outer dark.

"Nothing's more important than duty," said Ian, half to himself, his voice thoughtful and remote.

"Mercenary troops have the right to care and protection from their own officers. When they don't get it, they're entitled to justice, so that the same thing is discouraged from happening again. That justice is a duty."

Tyburn blinked, and unexpectedly a wall seemed to go down in his mind.

"Justice for those thirty-two dead soldiers of Brian's!" he said, suddenly understanding. "That's what brought you here!"

"Yes." Ian nodded, and lifted his glass almost as if to the sleet-ghosts to drink the rest of his whisky.

"But," said Tyburn, staring at him, "You're trying to bring a civilian to justice. And Kenebuck has you out-gunned and out-maneuvered—"

The chiming of the communicator screen in one corner of the hotel room interrupted him. Ian put down his empty glass, went over to the screen and depressed a stud. His wide shoulders and back hid the screen from Tyburn, but Tyburn heard his voice.

"Yes?"

The voice of James Kenebuck sounded in the hotel room.

"Graeme—listen!"

There was a pause.

"I'm listening," said Ian, calmly.

"I'm alone now," said the voice of Kenebuck. It was tight and harsh. "My guests have gone home. I was just looking through that package of Brian's things . . ." He stopped speaking and the sentence seemed to Tyburn to dangle unfinished in the air of the hotel room. Ian let it dangle for a long moment.

"Yes?" he said, finally.

"Maybe I was a little hasty . . ." said Kenebuck.

But the tone of his voice did not match the words. The tone was savage. "Why don't you come up, now that I'm alone, and we'll . . . talk about Brian, after all?"

"I'll be up," said Ian.

He snapped off the screen and turned around.

"Wait!" said Tyburn, starting up out of his chair. "You can't go up there!"

"Can't?" Ian looked at him. "I've been invited, Lieutenant."

The words were like a damp towel slapping Tyburn in the face, waking him up.

"That's right . . ." he stared at Ian. "Why? Why'd he invite you back?"

"He's had time," said Ian, "to be alone. And to look at that package of Brian's."

"But . . ." Tyburn scowled. "There was nothing important in that package. A watch, a wallet, a passport, some other papers . . . Customs gave us a list. There wasn't anything unusual there."

"Yes," said Ian. "And that's why he wants to see me again."

"But what does he want?"

"He wants me," said Ian. He met the puzzlement of Tyburn's gaze. "He was always jealous of Brian," Ian explained, almost gently. "He was afraid Brian would grow up to outdo him in things. That's why he tried to break Brian, even to kill him. But now Brian's come back to face him."

"Brian . . . ?"

"In me," said Ian. He turned toward the hotel door.

Tyburn watched him turn, then suddenly—like a man coming out of a daze, he took three hurried strides after him as Ian opened the door.

"Wait!" snapped Tyburn. "He won't be alone up there! He'll have hoods covering you through the walls. He'll definitely have traps set for you . . ."

Easily, Ian lifted the policeman's grip from his arm. "I know," he said. And went.

Tyburn was left in the open doorway, staring after him. As Ian stepped into the elevator tube, the policeman moved. He ran for the service elevator that would take him back to the police observation post above the sensors in the ceiling of Kenebuck's living room.

When Ian stepped into the foyer the second time, it was empty. He went to the door to the living room of Kenebuck's suite, found it ajar, and stepped through it. Within the room was empty, with glasses and overflowing ashtrays still on the tables; the lights had been lowered. Kenebuck rose from a chair with its back to the far, large window at the end of the room. Ian walked toward him and stopped when they were little more than an arm's length apart.

Kenebuck stood for a second, staring at him, the skin of his face tight. Then he made a short almost angry gesture with his right hand. The gesture gave away the fact that he had been drinking.

"Sit down!" he said. Ian took a comfortable chair and Kenebuck sat down in the one from which he had just risen. "Drink?" said Kenebuck. There was a decanter and glasses on the table beside and between them. Ian shook his head. Kenebuck poured part of a glass for himself.

"That package of Brian's things," he said, abruptly, the whites of his eyes glinting as he glanced up under his lids at Ian, "there was just personal stuff. Nothing else in it!"

"What else did you expect would be in it?" asked Ian, calmly.

Kenebuck's hands clenched suddenly on the glass.

He stared at Ian, and then burst out into a laugh that rang a little wildly against the emptiness of the large room.

"No, no . . ." said Kenebuck, loudly. "I'm asking the questions, Graeme. I'll ask them! What made you come all the way here, to see me, anyway?"

"My duty," said Ian.

"Duty? Duty to whom—Brian?" Kenebuck looked as if he would laugh again, then thought better of it. There was the white, wild flash of his eyes again. "What was something like Brian to you? You said you didn't even like him."

"That was beside the point," said Ian, quietly. "He was one of my officers."

"One of your officers! He was my brother! That's more than being one of your officers!"

"Not," answered Ian in the same voice, "where justice is concerned."

"Justice?" Kenebuck laughed. "Justice for Brian? Is that it?"

"And for thirty-two enlisted men."

"Oh—" Kenebuck snorted laughingly. "Thirty-two men . . . those thirty-two men!" He shook his head. "I never knew your thirty-two men, Graeme, so you can't blame me for them. That was Brian's fault; him and his idea—what was the charge they tried him on? Oh, yes, that he and his thirty-two or thirty-six men could raid enemy Headquarters and come back with the enemy Commandant. Come back . . . covered with glory." Kenebuck laughed again. "But it didn't work. Not my fault."

"Brian did it," said Ian, "to show you. You were what made him do it."

"Me? Could I help it if he never could match up to me?" Kenebuck stared down at his glass and took a quick swallow from it then went back to cuddling it in his hands. He smiled a little to himself. "Never could even *catch* up to me." He looked whitely across at Ian. "I'm just a better man, Graeme. You better remember that."

Ian said nothing. Kenebuck continued to stare at him; and slowly Kenebuck's face grew more savage.

"Don't believe me, do you?" said Kenebuck, softly. "You better believe me. I'm not Brian, and I'm not bothered by Dorsais. You're here, and I'm facing you —alone."

"Alone?" said Ian. For the first time Tyburn, above the ceiling over the heads of the two men, listening and watching through hidden sensors, thought he heard a hint of emotion—contempt—in Ian's voice. Or had he imagined it?

"Alone—Well!" James Kenebuck laughed again, but a little cautiously. "I'm a civilized man, not a hick frontiersman. But I don't have to be a fool. Yes, I've got men covering you from behind the walls of the room here. I'd be stupid not to. And I've got this . . ." He whistled, and something about the size of a small dog, but made of smooth, black metal, slipped out from behind a sofa nearby and slid on an aircushion over the carpeting to their feet.

Ian looked down. It was a sort of satchel with an orifice in the top from which two metallic tentacles protruded slightly.

Ian nodded slightly.

"A medical mech," he said.

"Yes," said Kenebuck, "cued to respond to the heartbeats of anyone in the room with it. So you see, it wouldn't do you any good, even if you somehow knew where all my guards were and beat them to the draw. Even if you killed me, this could get to me in time to keep it from being permanent. So, I'm unkillable. Give up!" He laughed and kicked at the mech. "Get back," he said to it. It slid back behind the sofa.

"So you see . . ." he said. "Just sensible precautions. There's no trick to it. You're a military man—and what's that mean? Superior strength. Superior tactics. That's all. So I outpower your strength, outnumber you, make your tactics useless—and what are you? Nothing." He put his glass carefully aside on the table with the decanter. "But I'm not Brian. I'm not afraid of you. I could do without these things if I wanted to."

Ian sat watching him. On the floor above, Tyburn had stiffened.

"Could you?" asked Ian.

Kenebuck stared at him. The white face of the millionaire contorted. Blood surged up into it, darkening it. His eyes flashed whitely.

"What're you trying to do—test me?" he shouted suddenly. He jumped to his feet and stood over Ian, waving his arms furiously. It was, recognized Tyburn overhead, the calculated, self-induced hysterical rage of the hoodlum world. But how would Ian Graeme below know that? Suddenly, Kenebuck was screaming. "You want to try me out? You think I won't face you? You think I'll back down like that brother of mine, that . . ." he broke into a flood of obscenity in which the name of Brian was freely mixed. Abruptly, he whirled about to the walls of the room, yelling at them. "Get out of there! All right, out! Do you hear me? All of you! Out—"

Panels slid back, bookcases swung aside and four men stepped into the room. Three were those who had been in the foyer earlier when Ian had entered for the first time. The other was of the same type.

"Out!" screamed Kenebuck at them. "Everybody

out. Outside, and lock the door behind you. I'll show this Dorsai, this . . ." almost foaming at the mouth, he lapsed into obscenity again.

Overhead, above the ceiling, Tyburn found himself gripping the edge of the table below the observation screen so hard his fingers ached.

"It's a trick!" he muttered between his teeth to the unhearing Ian. "He planned it this way! Can't you see that?"

"Graeme armed?" inquired the police sensor technician at Tyburn's right. Tyburn jerked his head around momentarily to stare at the technician.

"No," said Tyburn. "Why?"

"Kenebuck is." The technician reached over and tapped the screen, just below the left shoulder of Kenebuck's jacket image. "Slug-thrower."

Tyburn made a fist of his aching right fingers and softly pounded the table before the screen in frustration.

"All right!" Kenebuck was shouting below, turning back to the still-seated form of Ian, and spreading his arms wide. "Now's your chance. Jump me! The door's locked. You think there's anyone else near to help me? Look!" He turned and took five steps to the wide, knee-high to ceiling window behind him, punched the control button and watched as it swung wide. A few of the whirling sleet-ghosts outside drove from out of ninety stories of vacancy, into the opening—and fell dead in little drops of moisture on the windowsill as the automatic weather shield behind the glass blocked them out.

He stalked back to Ian, who had neither moved nor changed expression through all this. Slowly, Kenebuck sank back down into his chair, his back to the night, the blocked-out cold and the sleet.

"What's the matter?" he asked, slowly, acidly. "You don't do anything? Maybe *you* don't have the nerve, Graeme?"

"We were talking about Brian," said Ian.

"Yes, Brian . . ." Kenebuck said, quite slowly. "He had a big head. He wanted to be like me, but no matter how he tried—how I tried to help him—he couldn't make it." He stared at Ian. "That's just the way, he never could make it—the way he decided to go into enemy lines when there wasn't a chance in the world. That's the way he was—a loser."

"With help," said Ian.

"What? What's that you're saying?" Kenebuck jerked upright in his chair.

"You helped him lose," Ian's voice was matter of fact. "From the time he was a young boy, you built him up to want to be like you—to take long chances and win. Only your chances were always safe bets, and his were as unsafe as you could make them."

Kenebuck drew in an audible, hissing breath.

"You've got a big mouth, Graeme!" he said, in a low, slow voice.

"You wanted," said Ian, almost conversationally, "to have him kill himself off. But he never quite did. And each time he came back for more, because he had it stuck into his mind, carved into his mind, that he wanted to impress you—even though by the time he was grown, he saw what you were up to. He knew, but he still wanted to make you admit that he wasn't a loser. You'd twisted him that way while he was growing up, and that was the way he grew."

"Go on," hissed Kenebuck. "Go on, big mouth."

"So, he went off-Earth and became a professional soldier," went on Ian, steadily and calmly. "Not because he was drafted like someone from Newton or a

235

born professional from the Dorsai, or hungry like one of the ex-miners from Coby. But to show you you were wrong about him. He found one place where you couldn't compete with him, and he must have started writing back to you to tell you about it—half rubbing it in, half asking for the pat on the back you never gave him.''

Kenebuck sat in the chair and breathed. His eyes were all one glitter.

"But you didn't answer his letters," said Ian. "I suppose you thought that'd make him desperate enough to finally do something fatal. But he didn't. Instead he succeeded. He went up through the ranks. Finally, he got his commission and made Force-Leader, and you began to be worried. It wouldn't be long, if he kept on going up, before he'd be above the field officer grades, and out of most of the actual fighting."

Kenebuck sat perfectly still, a little leaning forward. He looked almost as if he were praying, or putting all the force of his mind to willing that Ian finish what he had started to say.

"And so," said Ian, "on his twenty-third birthday— which was the day before the night on which he led his men against orders into the enemy area—you saw that he got this birthday card . . ." He reached into a side pocket of his civilian jacket and took out a white, folded card that showed signs of having been savagely crumpled but was now smoothed out again. Ian opened it and laid it beside the decanter on the table between their chairs, the sketch and legend facing Kenebuck. Kenebuck's eyes dropped to look at it.

The sketch was a crude outline of a rabbit, with a combat rifle and battle helmet discarded at its feet, engaged in painting a broad yellow stripe down the center of its own back. Underneath this picture was printed in block letters, the question—"WHY FIGHT IT?"

Kenebuck's face slowly rose from the sketch to face Ian, and the millionaire's mouth stretched at the corners, and went on stretching into a ghastly version of a smile.

"Was that all . . . ?" whispered Kenebuck.

"Not all," said Ian. "Along with it, glued to the paper by the rabbit, there was this—"

He reached almost casually into his pocket.

"No, you don't!" screamed Kenebuck triumphantly. Suddenly he was on his feet, jumping behind his chair, backing away toward the darkness of the window behind him. He reached into his jacket and his hand came out holding the slug-thrower, which cracked loudly in the room. Ian had not moved, and his body jerked to the heavy impact of the slug.

Suddenly, Ian had come to life. Incredibly, after being hammered by a slug, the shock of which should have immobilized an ordinary man, Ian was out of the chair on his feet and moving forward. Kenebuck screamed again—this time with pure terror—and began to back away, firing as he went.

"Die, you—! Die!" he screamed. But the towering Dorsai figure came on. Twice it was hit and spun clear around by the heavy slugs, but like a football fullback shaking off the assaults of tacklers, it plunged on, with great strides narrowing the distance between it and the retreating Kenebuck.

Screaming finally, Kenebuck came up with the back of his knees against the low sill of the open window. For a second his face distorted itself out of all human shape in a grimace of its terror. He looked, to right and to left, but there was no place left to run. He had been pulling the trigger of his slugthrower all this time, but

237

now the firing pin clicked at last upon an empty chamber. Gibbering, he threw the weapon at Ian, and it flew wide of the driving figure of the Dorsai, now almost upon him, great hands outstretched.

Kenebuck jerked his head away from what was rushing toward him. Then, with a howl like a beaten dog, he turned and flung himself through the window before those hands could touch him, into ninety-odd stories of unsupported space. And his howl carried away down into silence.

Ian halted. For a second he stood before the window, his right hand still clenched about whatever it was he had pulled from his pocket. Then, like a toppling tree, he fell.

—As Tyburn and the technician with him finished burning through the ceiling above and came dropping through the charred opening into the room. They almost landed on the small object that had come rolling from Ian's now-lax hand. An object that was really two objects glued together. A small paint-brush and a transparent tube of glaringly yellow paint.

"I hope you realize, though," said Tyburn, two weeks later on an icy, bright December day as he and the recovered Ian stood just inside the Terminal waiting for the boarding signal from the spaceliner about to take off for the Sirian worlds, "what a chance you took with Kenebuck. It was just luck it worked out for you the way it did."

"No," said Ian. He was as apparently emotionless as ever; a little more gaunt from his stay in the Manhattan hospital, but he had mended with the swiftness of his Dorsai constitution. "There was no luck. It all happened the way I planned it."

Tyburn gazed in astonishment.

"Why . . ." he said, "if Kenebuck hadn't had to send his hoods out of the room to make it seem necessary for him to shoot you himself when you put your hand into your pocket that second time—or if you hadn't had the card in the first place—" He broke off, suddenly thoughtful. "You mean . . . ?" he stared at Ian. "Having the card, you planned to have Kenebuck get you alone . . . ?"

"It was a form of personal combat," said Ian. "And personal combat is my business. You assumed that Kenebuck was strongly entrenched, facing my attack. But it was the other way around."

"But you had to come to him—"

"I had to appear to come to him," said Ian, almost coldly. "Otherwise he wouldn't have believed that he had to kill me—before I killed him. By his decision to kill me, he put himself in the attacking position."

"But he had all the advantages!" said Tyburn, his head whirling. "You had to fight on his ground, here where he was strong . . ."

"No," said Ian. "You're confusing the attack position with the defensive one. By coming here, I put Kenebuck in the position of finding out whether I actually had the birthday card, and the knowledge of why Brian had gone against orders into enemy territory that night. Kenebuck planned to have his men in the foyer shake me down for the card—but they lost their nerve."

"I remember," murmured Tyburn.

"Then, when I handed him the package, he was sure the card was in it. But it wasn't," went on Ian. "He saw his only choice was to give me a situation where I might feel it was safe to admit having the card and the knowledge. He had to know about that, because Brian had called his bluff by going out and risking his neck after getting the card. The fact Brian was tried and executed later made no difference to Kenebuck. That was a matter of law—something apart from hoodlum guts, or lack of guts. If no one knew that Brian was braver than his older brother, that was all right; but if I knew, he could only save face under his own standards by killing me."

"He almost did," said Tyburn. "Any one of those slugs—"

"There was the medical mech," said Ian, calmly. "A man like Kenebuck would be bound to have something like that around to play safe—just as he would be bound to set an amateur's trap." The boarding horn of the spaceliner sounded. Ian picked up his luggage bag. "Good-by," he said, offering his hand to Tyburn.

"Good-by . . ." he muttered. "So you were just going along with Kenebuck's trap, all of it. I can't believe it . . ." He released Ian's hand and watched as the big man swung around and took the first two strides away toward the bulk of the ship shining in the winter sunlight. Then, suddenly, the numbness broke clear from Tyburn's mind. He ran after Ian and caught at his arm. Ian stopped and swung half-around, frowning slightly.

"I can't believe it!" cried Tyburn. "You mean you went up there, *knowing* Kenebuck was going to pump you full of slugs and maybe kill you—all just to square things for thirty-two enlisted soldiers under the command of a man you didn't even like? I don't believe it —you can't be that cold-blooded! I don't care how much of a man of the military you are!"

Ian looked down at him. And it seemed to Tyburn that the Dorsai face had gone away from him, somehow become as remote and stony as a face carved high up on some icy mountain's top.

"But I'm not just a man of the military," Ian said. "That was the mistake Kenebuck made, too. That was why he thought that stripped of military elements, I'd be easy to kill."

Tyburn, looking at him, felt a chill run down his spine as icy as wind off a glacier.

"Then, in heaven's name," cried Tyburn. "What are you?"

Ian looked from his far distance down into Tyburn's eyes and the sadness rang as clear in his voice finally, as iron-shod heels on barren rock.

"I am a man of war," said Ian, softly.

With that, he turned and went on; and Tyburn saw him black against the winter-bright sky, looming over all the other departing passengers, on his way to board the spaceship.

The Plume and the Sword
by
Sandra Miesel

◆

"Fantasy abandoned by reason produces impossible monsters; united with it, she is the mother of the arts and origin of marvels."

—Goya

In life even as in art, the harmony of opposites is Gordon R. Dickson's constant goal. This man who unifies opposing principles in his fiction unites within himself the most disparate extremes of frivolity and keenness—the plume and sword alike are his to wear.

In person, Dickson's fluffiness has always made the greatest impression on the greatest number of people. He is everyone's favorite conventioneer. (During his forty years in sf fandom, he has attended hundreds of conventions.) His image as the jolly party-goer, singing and playing the guitar until dawn, led Ben Bova to parody *My Darling Clementine* in Dickson's honor. The chorus concludes: "Science fiction is his hobby/ But his main job's having fun."

Dickson is a veteran trencherman, a mainstay of epic dinner parties, but he has also been known to spend more time selecting the wine than eating the meal. His bizarre preference for drinking milk, juice, coffee, beer, and Bloody Marys at the same breakfast has been cause for comment since his student days at the University of Minnesota thirty years ago. Lately, allergies (including—alas—a mild one to wine) and a desire for waistline trimness have tempered these habits somewhat, but Dickson's zest for living remains uncommonly brisk.

Yet such pleasures are the least components of his *joie de vivre*. Dickson has a capacity for wonder that will not be worn out. It has been claimed that no one else can say "golly" quite as joyfully as he does. (Dickson's habit of burbling along in innocent schoolboy exclamations once inspired some of his friends to stage a "Gordon R. Dickson Murfle-Alike Contest.")

Enthusiasm colors everything he does. He not only admires fine craftsmanship, he quizzes craftsmen on the tools, techniques, and attitudes that support their skills. (How many men would demand to see the wrong side of embroidered fabric?) He is always eager for new knowledge and fresh experiences. Recent endeavors include lessons in bagpipe-playing and in *akido*. Moreover, he encourages the same adventurousness in others. His friends have found themselves wielding knives, making lace, or writing novels for the first time at his urging.

Dickson describes himself as "a galloping optimist," unshakably certain that "man's future is onward and upward." Right must inevitably triumph. He admits that human beings may not be quite perfectible—"Perfectible is a little too good to be true—but improvable, tremendously improvable by their own strength."

Idealism gives him confidence in his own potential as well as that of his species. After watching his own Childe Cycle gradually move from rejection to acceptance, after observing fractious humans slowly struggle to build things together, Dickson concludes that creativity can overcome all obstacles. It is the only sure key to progress.

This same confidence in creativity makes him patient with other people, no matter how unpromising they may seem. He is among the most approachable of all sf professionals. For instance, few others would have taken the time to explain the elementary rules of prosody to an aspiring ballad writer and then been on hand afterwards to applaud her first acceptable efforts. Dickson's forbearance, skill, and above all, his respect for even the grubbiest amateur's dignity, have made him a superb mentor for young authors who are serious about their art. (Among the newer names in sf who have at times listened to him are Joe Haldeman, Robert Aspirin, and Lynn Abbey.) Dickson tends to downplay his influence because he believes that "fine teaching comes as automatically as breathing" to experienced writers. Yet his inner nature is revealed by the positive effects he has on those around him. For the past three decades his encouragement of talent and his support of professionalism have worked like buds of yeast to leaven the sf field.

One thing Dickson will not endure patiently is a shoddy performance. His Victorian upbringing imbued him with high standards of excellence. He has a born aristocrat's awareness of his own prerogatives, even in trivial matters: woe to the careless waiter who serves Dickson's vichyssoise improperly chilled. But his special ire is reserved for time-wasters too lazy to develop their own talents. "Some people," he complains, "like my advice so much, they frame it and hang it on the wall instead of using it." Fortunately such failures are rare. Most of those who beseech his advice or cry on his broad shoulders put the experience to good use.

Dickson's helpfulness arouses a corresponding helpfulness in others. Whether he asks for a Puritan sermon text, an Italian menu, a sample of Gregorian chant, or medical data on battle wounds, someone will promptly provide it—fandom is a living data bank. So grateful is he for help, he attracts almost too much solicitude. At times the attentiveness of friends reduces Dickson to the status of a favorite teddy bear in danger of having all its fur petted off.

Dickson's admirers do react intensely. Women's tears over the fate of Ian Graeme in *Soldier, Ask Not* prodded him to re-examine the implications of his text and see a solution to the tragedy. Other fans want to elaborate the Cycle's background with or without the author's sanction. There was the lawyer who speculated on interstellar legal systems and the artist who tried to predict future art tastes. The most conspicuous example of this phenomenon is a non-profit organization known as the Dorsai Irregulars which provides security services at sf conventions, sometimes in costume. The author has licensed their use of the Dorsai name and insignia.

Dickson appreciates such vivid identification because he enjoys playing roles himself. The historical persona he designed to join the Society for Creative Anachronism is "Kenneth of Otterburn," a fourteenth-century border lord whose heraldic badge is the otter. This character is a bow to duality in general and to Dickson's own Anglo-Scottish heritage in particular. One earlier member of his family, Simon Fraser, the eleventh Lord Lovat, was beheaded in 1747 for supporting Bonnie Prince Charlie. The official Dickson crest is: "a hart couchant gardant proper; attired, or within two branches of laurel leaves vert in orle," which is to say, a stag with gilded horns at rest on a field bordered with green laurel leaves. The family motto is *"Cubo sed curo,"* "I lie down but I remain watchful."

More importantly, this SCA project, like so many of

Dickson's activities, is a remote preparation for the Childe Cycle. The climax of *Childe,* the concluding volume of the series, will be modeled on the Battle of Otterburn fought between the English and the Scots in 1388. Furthermore, investigating the life of an imaginary medieval nobleman will also give the author special insights into the mind of the real Sir John Hawkwood, hero of the Cycle's planned opening volume.

Dickson is never content to do his research from books, even from primary sources. Whenever possible, he must visit sites and handle actual artifacts. For example, he absorbs historical *mana* by fingering Plantagenet coins and reading gothic manuscripts. When reality is unattainable, he turns to replicas. His most ambitious plan yet is to commission the making of a complete suit of armor such as Hawkwood might have worn. (He rejects suggestions that experiments with fleas, lice, and dysentery might be equally instructive.) So far, he has acquired only the mailshirt, helmet, and a magnificent pair of armored gloves. But attired in a friend's full equippage, Dickson cut a marvelously gallant figure—six feet of russet-haired, blue-eyed knight with a bit of lace visible at his wrist to accent the steel and leather. "I feel as if I could walk through doors," he proclaimed, striding off down the motel corridor. Fortunately, no other guests disputed his passage.

But his own experience did not suffice. He wanted to observe another man's reactions as well. So he convinced a less-than-eager Kelly Freas to try on the armor next. Freas, being shorter and stockier, probably approximated a real medieval knight better than Dickson. Others might have followed suit, but by then the outfit's undergarments were disagreeably drenched with sweat. The author's zeal for medieval weaponry is so compelling that on another occasion he insisted that one notably unmartial colleague take up arms and beat on the maple trees in Dickson's back yard with a sword—all by way of sealing a business partnership.

Although mimetic research sounds amusing, it is no game to Dickson but rather a measure of his dedication to his craft. He needs to set all his senses gathering data in order to generate the authentic details his writing requires. His creativity is almost a metabolic process: information digested, art synthesized. Consider the awesome volume of material he had to process for *The Far Call,* the finest realistic novel about the space program yet written. This book's flavor comes from the author's own fervent pro-space views. Its substance is the product of many visits to Kennedy Space Center and lengthy consultations with experts on the scene. Dickson believes he must eat the bread of a place before he can truly know it.

Dickson deliberately incorporates his own interests, experiences, and values in his fiction. Take, for instance, his fascination with animal psychology. "I tend to gestalt things," he says. "I see humans and animals as illuminating one another by what they do and also humans and animals illuminating aliens and vice versa." Thus Dickson's favorite beasts show up in his pages, either wearing their own hides or disguised as extraterrestrials: bears *(Spacial Delivery, The Alien Way),* wolves *(Sleepwalker's World),* sea mammals *(Home From the Shore, The Space Swimmers),* cats *(Time Storm, The Masters of Everon),* and, of course, otters *(Alien Art).* On the other hand, Dickson lent his own antic enthusiasm and exasperating glee to the teddy bear-like Hokas *(Earthman's Burden, Star Prince Charlie*

written with his old college classmate Poul Anderson).
Dickson contemplating a gourmet meal or a fine guitar
is the very image of a Hoka.

Guitar in hand, Dickson is a pillar of convention
"filksings," gatherings of people who perform odd
songs which may or may not have any bearing on sf.
Although his tenor has lost its original clarity, his ren-
ditions of classics like *The Face on the Barroom Floor* or
The Three Ravens are still enjoyable. It is even more of
a treat to hear him sing his own compositions like the
grim *Battle Hymn* of the Friendlies, the wistful love song
from *Necromancer*, or the rollicking *Ballad of the Shoshonu*.
This has inspired some of his fans to write Childe Cycle songs themselves.

Among sf writers, Dickson is second only to Poul
Anderson in the ornamental use of songs and poetry.
Like Anderson, Dickson was raised on folk ballads,
epics, fairy tales, and the great nineteenth-century
novels, although there was more of a British than a
Scandinavian slant to his literary formation. Furthermore, Dickson along with Anderson, Robert A.
Heinlein, Jerry Pournelle, Richard McKenna, John
Brunner, and Cordwainer Smith, has been heavily in-
fluenced by Rudyard Kipling. (Kipling's impact on sf,
now reaching into its second and third generation, has
never been adequately investigated.) However,
Dickson also cites major mainstream American and
Russian authors and even Thomas Mann among his
influences.

One expects a professional writer to maintain a
large library and, indeed, the walls of Dickson's Rich-
field, Minnesota home are lined with books. But
Dickson is a true bibliophile. He loves books simply as
physical objects, delighting in fine bindings and crisp
pages. He shows a marked preference for hardbound

volumes even for works of passing interest. Accompanying him to a bookstore is like tagging behind a tornado. His ever-expanding holdings are systematically catalogued and he maintains a complete collection of his own editions.

Dickson has stronger opinions than most writers on how his work should be illustrated and collects originals of the illustrations that please him. (Wallspace in his home not devoted to books is mostly covered with art.) His feeling for visual aesthetics was deepened by years of night classes at the Minneapolis Institute of Arts. His studies taught him the difference between written and painted visions. As he ruefully observes, too often writers try to paint with their "writing equipment" while painters try to write with their "painting equipment."

Dickson's life and career are also molded by a complementary set of physical pursuits. Allergies—and time—now bar him from the camping, climbing, and other outdoor recreations he formerly enjoyed. However, on a recent trip to Florida he caught the small marlin that decorates his office wall. Still, the experiences he has had with wildlife and open spaces remain with him as raw material for creative efforts. He would not be the same man or the same writer if boyhood memories of Pacific breakers did not echo in his dreams.

Dickson's handling of nature is subtler than Anderson's lush, almost pantheistic approach. He sees it primarily as a milieu for human action. (His preference for somber, austere landscapes is most sensitively revealed in *Alien Art*.) Having lived in Western Canada as a child and in Minnesota since prompts his frequent use of these regions as story settings, either directly or as models for alien worlds. His beloved Canadian mountains, "the bones of the continent," become the cool, rocky highlands of the Dorsai. Northcountry lakes and woodlands reappear in *Pro*.

Indoors, Dickson's ardor for fitness shames his more sedentary friends. His ambition to achieve something of the high performance under stress he admires in tough old fighting men like Hawkwood led to his involvement with the martial arts—the chivalry of medieval Europe and the *bushido* of feudal Japan have much in common. Formal training has done more than impart special physical skills. It has also reinforced views he already held on self-mastery and functional beauty. Performing a clean knife pass takes the discipline of a dancer; a well-designed blade is a pleasing piece of metal sculpture.

Dickson uses the Oriental martial arts to study the attainment and control of that perennially fascinating phenomenon, the exaltation state. He can and on occasion has discussed the topic for long hours on end. What lies behind hysterical strength, stunning intuition, heroic virtue? Creativity is once again his answer. When human beings operate at the very highest levels their bodies, minds, or spirits permit, they enter a transcendant phase Dickson calls "creative overdrive." In this condition, they can direct their conscious and unconscious powers to some otherwise unreachable goal. Salvation is integration and creativity integrates.

Thus, cerebral, artistic adventure heroes are Dickson's specialty. For instance, in *The Final Encyclopedia*, Hal Mayne is a poet who has passed through previous incarnations as a soldier (*Dorsai!*) and a mystic (*Necromancer*). Michael de Sandoval in *Lost Dorsai* is a musician and Cletus Grahame in *Tactics of Mistake* has tried painting. Dickson endows his heroes with the talents he himself esteems and lets them demonstrate overdrive by their deeds. They are offered as examples of what the entire race could achieve if only its creative energies were fully liberated.

Dickson himself is an advertisement for his theories. His memory lapses are legendary—once when making introductions, he could not recall his own brother's name. He often confuses the titles of his books, scrambles the locations of his planets, and forgets the lyrics to his own songs. Nevertheless, his mind becomes astonishingly supple and efficient when overdrive directs it in the service of his art. In this heightened state, he can move briskly through public appearances though exhausted and can soar to fresh imaginative insights. For Dickson, creativity is both the journey and the journey's end. It enables him to unite the plumy and swordlike extremes of his own nature in order to work.

He has an unparalleled sense of vocation, a commitment to his artistic mission as keen as any crusader's vow. By writing the Cycle, he hopes to bring the evolutionary progress he describes that much closer. When asked if he expects the Childe Cycle to appear on some thirtieth century list of Ten Books That Changed the Cosmos, Dickson replied with a smile, "And what are the other nine?" His idealism has been dismissed as naive in some quarters but events within and without the sf field continue to vindicate him.

Some authors stumble into their trade for lack of anything better to do; others are forced into it by economic necessity. Not so Dickson: "I've been a writer all my life, as far back as I can remember. Nobody ever told me not to until later on, by which time it was too late." His talents were encouraged by his parents, an Australian-born mining engineer and an American school teacher who met and married in Canada. His older half-brother is the distinguished Canadian novelist Lovat Dickson, but his mother's influence was the crucial formative one. Her reading him books and telling him stories are among his fondest early memories.

Maude Dickson, a wonderfully gracious and spry lady of ninety-one, modestly disputes the importance of her efforts. Nevertheless, her son was a precocious writer: a newspaper published his poem "Apple Blossoms" when he was only seven years old. In 1939, at age fifteen, he entered the University of Minnesota to major in creative writing but his studies were interrupted by military service during World War II. Army aptitude tests predicted he would have a bright future as a dentist.

Dickson graduated in 1948, planning to take his doctorate, teach, and write on the side. He abandoned this "unduly sensible" scheme to follow his gift and write full-time. It was a desperate gamble. He supported himself by selling his blood—twice as often as permitted—and subsisted on a diet of stale bread, peanut butter, and vitamin pills. His sacrifices were rewarded when his first sf story, "The Friendly Man," appeared in *Astounding* in February, 1951.

Three decades, 40 novels, and 175 shorter works later, the gamble may be said to have paid off in honors and prosperity. Dickson has won the Hugo for "Soldier, Ask Not" (1965), the Nebula for "Call Him Lord" (1966), the Jupiter for *Time Storm* (1977), and the British Fantasy Award for *The Dragon and the George* (1978) as well as receiving many other award nominations. These days, a dedicated staff including a full-time business manager and part-time secretarial and research workers assist him. Maintaining his affairs in good order requires an otter-keeper's patience but the task should become easier once the intricacies of his newly purchased computer system are unraveled.

Dickson is one master who seeks perfection in his craft and freely shares his expertise with fellow guildsmen. He served two terms as President of the Science Fiction Writers of America (1969-71) and is currently working to extend the benefits of SFWA's organizational experience to the fledgling Association of Science Fiction Artists. Much in demand as a speaker and resource person, he is one of the few non-academic professional writers in the Science Fiction Research Association. He took part in one Clarion Workshop for new writers and regularly attended the Milford Conference for established writers during the 1960's. (However, he was never known as a member of the infamous "Milford Mafia.") He has also been invited to participate in sessions of the Science Fiction Institute, a teacher-training program held annually at the University of Kansas. Thus, chat by speech, he fosters professional excellence and public understanding.

Dickson's mastery of technique combines theoretical lessons acquired in university classes taught by such people as Sinclair Lewis and Robert Penn Warren with ruthlessly practical ones learned in the low-paying sf magazine market. His faith in his own ability saw him safely through both processes. "I was a fully-formed writer long before I got my degree," he explains. "I had enough mass and momentum along the road I wanted to travel so that I couldn't be jolted off." Neither lethal classroom situations nor the pressure of gaining enough story skills to stay alive blocked his progress.

Now in the mellowness of his maturity, Dickson is reaching the destination he chose for himself half a century ago. He successfully merges style and content, polished literary form and research-based substance, into one liquid whole. Although clarity can be a handicap when critics equate obscurity with profundity, Dickson's art conceals his artfulness on purpose with a view to reaching the widest possible audience. He believes that "good fiction should become transparent so people end up reading it not so much for the words as for the ideas."

Dickson has always been a highly conscious writer. There is nothing random or spontaneous in his tightly structured prose, never a wheel misplaced, never a gear unmeshed. He seeks the optimum configuration for his fictional drive train in order to transmit messages most efficiently. Philosophical convictions generate the relentless power of his best work.

He calls his method of rendering principles in fiction the "consciously thematic novel." This technique, developed from mainstream models, enables him to argue a specific point of view without resorting to propaganda. It presents an unbiased selection of natural incidents to support its thesis. "The aim is to make the theme such an integral part of the novel that it can be effective upon the reader without ever having to be stated explicitly," says Dickson. A consciously thematic story can, of course, be read and enjoyed for its entertainment value alone. But ideally, when the reader sees all the resonances and repetitions, the author hopes that "he will do the work of looking at this slew of evidence I've laid out and will, on his own, come to the conclusion I'd like him to reach."

Dickson calls the Childe Cycle "my showpiece for the consciously thematic novel." Curiously enough, the Cycle itself originated in this very way, through a deeper interpretation of pre-existing evidence—as though the unconscious side of the author's mind were operating on the conscious side via thematic methods.

During the 1940's, Dickson started—but never finished—an historical novel entitled *The Pikeman* about a young Swiss mercenary serving in fifteenth century Italy. This plot, enhanced by ideas drawn from Rafael Sabatini's *Bellarion* and from *Astounding* editor John W. Campbell, yielded *Dorsai!* in 1959. Then during the course of a night-time asthma attack at the following summer's Milford Conference, a hitherto unsuspected pattern sprang at Dickson from the pages of *Dorsai!*. "Eureka! I had it!" he recalls. "I got up the next morning and spent three hours trying to tell Richard McKenna about it, a process by which I sorted it out in my mind. The essential structure was born full-blown at that moment."

The Childe Cycle is an epic of human evolution, a scenario for mankind's rite of passage. Over the course of a thousand years, from the fourteenth century to the twenty-fourth, interactions between three archetypical Prime Characters—the Men of Faith, War, and Philosophy—succeed in uniting the unconscious/conservative and the conscious/progressive halves of the racial psyche. The result is a fully-evolved being endowed with intuition, empathy, and creativity whom Dickson calls Ethical-Responsible Man. At that point, the human organism will no longer be a "childe" but a spurred and belted knight.

In Dickson's future universe, mankind has shattered into Splinter Cultures that develop only one facet of human nature at the expense of the others. The most important Splinter Cultures are: the Dorsai (Warriors —Body), the Exotics (Philosophers—Mind), and the Friendlies (Believers—Spirit) but none of these is fully human and none has the ultimate society. Dickson's Messianic hero Donal Graeme, first-born of the

Ethical-Responsible Men, lives three lives and thereby absorbs the best qualities of Warrior, Philosopher, and Believer. His indomitable will divides the racial psyche in order to develop it, then reunites it in order to perfect it.

When completed, the Cycle will consist of three historical, three contemporary, and six science fiction novels. *Dorsai!* (1959), *Necromancer* (1960), *Soldier, Ask Not* (1968), and *Tactics of Mistake* (1971) have already appeared and are scheduled for reissue by Ace. *The Final Encyclopedia* and *Childe* are currently in preparation. These novels are accompanied by a series of shorter works or "illuminations" that stand outside the argument of the Cycle proper but share the same settings and characters: "Warrior" (1965), "Brothers" (1973), "Amanda Morgan" (1979) and *Lost Dorsai* (1980). "Amanda Morgan" and "Brothers" have been set in a narrative frame with illustrations and published by Ace as *The Spirit of Dorsai* (1979). Although each work can stand alone, it is even more enjoyable understood in proper context. The novels are best read in order of publication rather than according to internal chronology—one should begin with *Dorsai!* to follow Donal Graeme's forays backwards and forwards in time.

The illuminations must not be lumped together with the Cycle in one amorphous mass. There is no such thing as the "Dorsai series." Dickson's subject is mankind, not the Dorsai. Indiscriminate labeling also obscures the uniqueness of Dickson's plan. He is not writing a coherent future history in the manner of Robert A. Heinlein, Poul Anderson, Larry Niven, or Jerry Pournelle. Neither is he merely re-using a familiar universe the way Andre Norton and R.A. Lafferty do. Least of all is Dickson building alien planets like

Hal Clement or alien cultures like C. J. Cherryh.

Notice the vagueness of the chronology, the improbability of the colonial locales, and the essential familiarity of the environments thanks to terraforming. Dickson's universe is not wildly futuristic despite advanced military hardware and a few props like floating chairs. The interstellar flights shown might as well be intercontinental.

Compare Dickson's approach with the exoticism of Frank Herbert. Although *Dune* postdates *Dorsai!*, it, too, features a Messianic hero surrounded by equivalents of the Dorsai, the Exotics, and the Friendlies. Herbert clothes his philosophy in fabulously intricate costumes but Dickson presents his in sleekly functional garb to reveal the form beneath the fabric. In all respects, Dickson's universe is a selected reality, neither naturalistic nor fantastic.

Dickson has staunchly resisted pressure from enthusiastic readers to elaborate the Cycle's background. He introduces new details (such as Dorsai domestic arrangements in "Amanda Morgan") only as required to tell his story. For most of the two decades between *Dorsai!* and *The Final Encyclopedia*, he carried all his notes in his head. This bred a host of small inconsistencies, now purged from these Ace editions. The artistic energy that might have otherwise gone into constructing genealogies or inventing languages powers the illuminations instead. These short works enable the author to spotlight certain characters and events within the Cycle without disturbing its structure.

The illuminations serve many purposes. They dramatize events that are off-stage in the novels: Dorsai non-combatants repelling Earth's elite troops has to be taken on faith in *Tactics of Mistake* but "Amanda

Morgan" makes the defense convincing. They magnify incidents: Kensie's death is a mere plot device in *Dorsai!,* attains mythic stature in *Soldier, Ask Not,* and is finally depicted in "Brothers." They bring characters into focus: Corunna El Man has only a cameo role in *Dorsai!* but serves as the roving narrator of *Lost Dorsai* and may become the hero of his own illumination someday. Above all, they elucidate principles: "Warrior" reveals the values a true man of war will live and die for.

Each illumination examines the twin moral issues of integrity and responsibility: how can human beings reconcile what they must be with what they must do? The major arena of conflict is the will—notice how little space is actually devoted to physical combat. The stakes are higher in each succeeding contest because the fates of more people are at risk: a few individuals in "Warrior," a city in "Brothers," a planet in "Amanda Morgan," and all the inhabited worlds in *Lost Dorsai.* Victory must always be bought in blood because the willingness to die is the ultimate proof of commitment. Again and again, the ancient myth of the hero's saving death is played out among the stars. Martyrdom at the hands of enemies in the illuminations complements Donal's voluntary self-sacrifices in the Cycle.

"Warrior" grew from a tiny detail in *Dorsai!*—the terrible scar on Ian's arm. This earliest and simplest of the illuminations sets the pattern for those that followed. It proclaims that fidelity to ideals and duty will ultimately prevail, whatever the odds. Vice is always vulnerable because it cannot comprehend virtue's tactics.

"Warrior" makes explicit what *Dorsai!* only implied: one of Ian's special functions as the ultimate

Man of War is to avenge sins committed by and against warriors. In this story, set a decade before the opening of *Dorsai!*, Ian is still a young commandant. He punishes a reckless officer for wasting his men's lives, then destroys the culprit's gangster brother for goading him to hunt glory. Through Ian, the lone wolf facing mad dogs, Dickson defines the honorable and dishonorable uses of force.

Ian's triumph is shown through the eyes of Tyburn, a conscientious policeman who tries to protect Ian despite his civilian distaste for the military. The reader sees what Tyburn cannot: he, too, in his humble way is a righteous Defender. The proud gifts that bloom in the Dorsai still remain in the rootstock people of Earth. Bringing the potential in all persons to harvest, not glorifying supermen, is the Cycle's goal.

Dickson uses an ordinary man as a "lens of heroic experience" even more skillfully in "Brothers." This story's first person narrator is St. Marie police chief Tomas Velt. He brings the larger-than-life Graeme twins into scale and his reactions make the epic events surrounding Kensie's death believable. Tom is stubbornly normal. He knows his own limitations but does not let them paralyze him. His balance and dedication collide with the self-hatred and thoughtlessness of his best friend and symbolic brother Pel. Pel adores Kensie yet betrays him; Tom undervalues Ian yet aids him. Responsibility is the thread tying Tom to Ian. It makes him Ian's smaller counterpart just as Tyburn was in "Warrior." The policeman and the commander cooperate to find Kensie's assassins before Dorsai wrath falls on the city where the outrage occurred.

Ian's dilemma is the cruelest. He must uphold the Dorsai ideal of restraint and at the same time obtain justice for his slain brother. He risks his life rather

259

than his principles and so gains the victory. His grief for the brother who was his "other self" is measureless in its very silence, like a scream of agony pitched too low for human ears to hear. Initially, Ian shows "no more emotion at his brother's death than he might have on discovering an incorrect Order of the Day." Yet his wordless last farewell to Kensie is fierce enough to crumple steel—and spectators' hearts.

Though Ian is left to walk in darkness all his days, dying cannot dim Kensie's godlike radiance. In retrospect, his murder becomes a sacrifice for his death saves what it was meant to destroy. When the people of St. Marie mourn this beautiful dead Balder, they are cleansed by their own tears. Kensie becomes their adopted hero. By emulating him they will achieve the self-respect and self-control their "fat little farm world" had hitherto lacked. Furthermore, Kensie's assassination interlocks with the voluntary martyrdom of Jamethon Black, the Friendly officer who gives up his life to save his troops in *Soldier, Ask Not*. Both are victims of Tam Olyn, a vengeful Earthman who negates everything they stand for. Yet, in the end this Judas is redeemed, partly through the merits of Kensie, Jamethon, and Ian. When wholeness of heart unites with devotion to duty, nothing evil can endure.

"Amanda Morgan" is as resolutely feminine as "Brothers" is masculine. *The Spirit of Dorsai*'s two components fit together as smoothly as *yin* and *yang*, as naturally as root and blossom. Ian flourishes in the high summer of Dorsai. Amanda was already there at the first signs of spring. Though a century divides them, hero and heroine are complementary halves of the same defensive shield.

As her descendant Amanda III explains, Earth-born Amanda I "was Dorsai before there was a Dorsai world. What she was, was the material out of which our people and our culture here were made." Like the matriarch in *John Brown's Body*, Amanda builds her homestead "out of her blood and bone/ With her heart for the Hall's foundation-stone." She builds well. Her household, Fal Morgan, endures until the Splinter Cultures are no more.

This dynamic heroine makes "Amanda Morgan" a major landmark in Dickson's literary development. Women simply do not exist within the pages of "Brothers"—even its underlying myths are wholly male. However, in the six years following the original publication of "Brothers," Dickson taught himself step by step to expand this "collapsed area of the continuum." Tracing the course of his progress would be an essay in itself, but *The Spirit of Dorsai* is a fine yardstick to measure the gap covered.

Sex-role reversals abound in "Amanda Morgan" without shrieking for attention—this is art, not propaganda. No capital letters announce that the Dorsai world is a *de facto* matriarchy. Initially, women had to manage planetary affairs while their men were off to the wars. (The analogy to medieval chatelaines is obvious and intended.) As economic conditions improve, the proportion of soldiers in the population declines. By Ian's time, only a minority of Dorsai—women as well as men—are professional soldiers, but planetside women still guard the continuity of the culture.

Individual merit affects the pattern as much as necessity. While avoiding the fashionable error of belittling all males to exalt all females, this story allows men to be sensitive and women tough. Minor touches carry out the theme: a reckless young girl protects a smaller, shyer boy; formidable General Khan meekly prepares sandwiches. Major examples cluster around Amanda herself. In the colony's early days, she led the fight against outlaw gangs. Years later when Earth invades the Dorsai, she is still "the best person to command" her District—even at age ninety-two. Amanda personally defies the invaders' General Amorine. (Note the unconscious word play in their names.) Neither his legions nor his shiny hardware impress her, for her strength is that of family, hearth, and the living world.

Unconquerable Amanda is both memorable and complex. Although she is Dorsai through and through, she (and her namesakes the second and third Amandas) can believe, think, and fight like the fully evolved humans of the future. Yet she is not complacent about her own excellence. Self-criticism keeps her learning and growing in her tenth decade of life. In the course of the story she achieves new insights. She discovers that "you love what you give to—and in proportion as you give." (Ian lives by the reverse principle.) She realizes that the most loving thing an integrated and responsible person can do is allow others to master these virtues for themselves. She learns how to let go after a lifetime of holding fast.

"To strive and not to yield" might be the Dorsai motto: no power can break the Dorsai will. It is the capacity to resist Wrong that defines a Dorsai, not physical might. (The one Dorsai renegade mentioned is superbly gifted.) The Dorsai spirit blazes as brightly in crippled bodies as in sound ones, as purely in Amanda as in Ian. What Dorsai indomitability protects is the right to be free. This is their practical function in interstellar politics and their metaphysical function in racial evolution. Whether they die defending their homes or attacking on some foreign battlefield, Dorsai must buy their freedom with blood. These Defenders' readiness to die—and the tactical efficiency of their dying—is their margin of survival.

Lost Dorsai couples the willingness to die with the refusal to kill. This story demonstrates that a Dorsai can even be a pacifist without repudiating his cultural ideals. Tensions between integrity and responsibility are especially severe here because of the number of characters and the intertwined complexity of the difficulties they face.

Both Michael and the second Amanda are "afraid that their instincts would lead them to do what their thinking minds had told them they should not do." His problem is war, hers, love. Her dilemma entangles Kensie, the warrior who loves her and Ian, the warrior she loves. Michael's runs parallel to that of Corunna who lost his beloved in war.

All the knots pull tight during the siege of Gebel Nahar, a "few against the many" situation so typical of Dickson. (The siege of Earth in *The Final Encyclopedia* will be the ultimate example.) This military crisis is a symptom of grave social imbalances, not only in Nahar but on Ceta and all the inhabited worlds. The web tears at a single pull. Michael's sacrifice affects far more than the lives immediately around him. He adds a bit of impetus to the forces breaking humanity free from the net that confines it.

Every issue in *Lost Dorsai* shares a common factor: the cleavage between *being* and *doing*. The troubled groups and individuals shown cannot reconcile private essence with social existence. The Naharese are obsessed with the form rather than the substance of *el honor*. They have no valid ethic to bridle their violent impulses. This morbid culture points up the healthiness of the Dorsai. It also demonstrates that in the long run, all Splinter Cultures are too distorted to be viable. The Dorsai regard Naharese martial fantasies as obscene—empty and unreal as pornography. But their judgment may be too harsh. Even these comic-opera soldiers can respond to a genuine hero when one appears.

Michael renounced his Dorsai heritage rather than compromise his non-violent beliefs. Corunna has suppressed his feelings to bury himself in his work. The Conde is the ghost of an authority figure, not a man. His underlings prefer to keep their lives instead of their honor. Ian neglects his own needs in favor of the gestalt identity he shares with his twin. Kensie tries to attain his own dream without gauging the impact on Ian. Amanda is torn between the wish to belong to one person and the need to be available to many.

Padma is the only balanced personality in the cast and the only one without a quandary. This passive observer watches and learns but does not appear to grow inwardly during the ordeal. For one dedicated to evolutionary progress, he is curiously static. There is a greater irony in the fiery Conde's unslaked thirst for martyrdom. The cup of glory goes instead to Michael, who never desired it. Paradoxically, it is Michael's refusal of his original calling that positions him for an unprecedented adventure—no other Dorsai ever defeated an army singlehandedly.

Dickson allows his hero a grand ceremonial tribute after death. There is none in the story that inspired *Lost Dorsai*, Kipling's "Drums of the Fore and Aft" (1889). There two scruffy British drummer boys turn rout into victory by charging the Afghans alone, but all the recognition they get from their shamefaced regiment is an unmarked grave.

Michael's monument, the *Leto de muerte*, is a custom Dickson invented for this story. It was suggested by the practice of throwing prizes—even personal belongings

—to successful bullfighters, something he had witnessed during travels in Mexico. (Roman gladiators may have been rewarded in the same way.) He was not thinking of the mass sacrifices of battle trophies made by the Iron Age Celts, although the gestures are similar in spirit.

Dickson modeled quasi-Hispanic Nahar partly on Galicia. The Gallegos are the Scots or Bretons of Spain —a romantic but suspicious people. Their lean country is the ancient heart of Spain and the site of its holiest shrine, Santiago de Compostela. (Coincidentally, among Galicia's cities is La Coruña—medieval Corunna—from which the story's narrator takes his name.) However, Nahar's social conditions—hungry *campesinos* and greedy *ricones*—resemble those in contemporary Latin America. The Dorsai could easily be U.S. military advisers caught in a revolution. But the merits of the two warring parties are not really at issue. What matters is preventing the tyrant William from exploiting the situation to his own advantage. Cries for justice—in Nahar and elsewhere—will not be properly answered until the Cycle's close a century hence.

Since the moment of fulfillment is not yet at hand, partial solutions are all *Lost Dorsai*'s survivors can reach. Corunna's heart is just beginning to heal. (He will seem normal when he meets Donal Graeme in *Dorsai!*.) Whatever Padma has learned, it does not include a profound understanding of the Graeme twins. But having shared the Gebel Nahar experience with them may dispose him to act on their behalf in "Brothers." Losing Amanda weakens Kensie's will to live enough to doom him in "Brothers" about five years later. The excess of fraternal love Ian shows by refusing to compete with Kensie for Amanda is precisely why he suffers so much in "Brothers" and afterwards. Amanda strikes a better balance than the men. Though the Star Maiden grieves both her twin suitors, she does win peace of soul for herself. She becomes a spiritual mother to her people as the first Amanda was a physical one.

Only Michael's victory is final because it is sealed in death. Michael is a willing sacrificial lamb. Kensie is a bright golden Achilles cut down in his prime. Ian, on the other hand, endures like a battered Herakles. He is the ultimate Dorsai, with a darkness in him so deep it bedazzles. He demonstrates how much harder it is to *live* heroically than to *die* heroically. Not for Ian the quick, sharp moment of trial. He must prove himself day in and day out through one grim moral choice after another. His leadership and example help the Dorsai survive desperate times. Thus something remains of his family and people a century later for Hal Mayne and his beloved, the third Amanda, to use in the evolutionary struggle.

Thus the illuminations, like the Childe Cycle they complement, turn on the question of balance. Though the demands of integrity and responsibility can clash, they should unite to reinforce each other. As the second Amanda concludes: " 'In the end the only way is to be what you are and do what you must. If you do that, everything works.' " Balance through union is a universal imperative for the race as well as the individual. The conscious and unconscious aspects of human nature must come together. Then evolved mankind—intuitive, empathic, creative—can win the future without losing the past.

To dramatize these principles, Dickson has in effect assembled his own set of secular-historical archetypes. The Cycle and the illuminations function like an original system of mythology that correlates with nearly every area of human experience. It has shaped the author as much as he has shaped it: life anticipates art; art elucidates life. Dickson could apply Hopkins' definition to himself: "What I do is me: for that I came." His twenty-year quest to complete the Childe Cycle has become a kind of initiation for him, both as an artist and as a man. He tried to live the unity he preaches by combining fluffy and intense traits within himself. He knows that separately, the plume is frivolous and the sword ruthless. But together they are gallant.

The plume waves. The sword flashes. The proud chevalier has pledged himself to see the journey through and will not count the cost of keeping faith.

Editor's note: *As a special bonus for readers of* Lost Dorsai, *the author has consented to the publication of an extensive excerpt from his great work-in-progress,* The Final Encyclopedia. *Penultimate novel in the Childe Cycle, Mr. Dickson feels that* The Final Encyclopedia *is his most significant work to date. It commences on the following page.*

THE FINAL ENCYCLOPEDIA: AN EXCERPT

The story up to this point:

Hal Mayne, an orphan found in a small, otherwise empty interstellar ship drifting near Earth orbit, is raised on Earth by three tutors, who are his guardians: one Dorsai, one Exotic, and one Friendly.

When he is fifteen years old his guardians are murdered by the Others, the ambitious and charismatic crossbreeds of the Splinter Cultures, who are rapidly gaining control of human societies throughout all the inhabited worlds. The historical time is approximately 100 years after the time of Dorsai! and Soldier, Ask Not.

Such a contingency had been foreseen by the tutors. Hal, grown, will be the natural opponent of the crossbreeds, but until grown he is no match for them. He flees, first to Coby, the mining world where he spends nearly two years, until he is located there by the Others—although the Others still do not realize his potential. Still, their second in command, Nigel Blas, has become interested enough to want to see Hal face to face.

Hal escapes from Coby and lands on Harmony, under the alias of a dead Friendly known as Howard Immanuelson. Recalcitrants are opposing the Others and their controlled governments on both Harmony and Association. As Immanuelson, Hal is befriended by a recalcitrant named Jason Rowe, whom Hal meets in the detention center where both Jason and he are being held by the local authorities under the suspicion of their being what Jason actually is.

THE FINAL ENCYCLOPEDIA:
An Excerpt

The cell door clashed open, waking them. Instinctively, Hal Mayne was on his feet by the time the guard came through the open door and he saw out of the corner of his eye that Jason Rowe was also.

"All right," said the guard. He was thin and tall—though not as tall as Hal—with a starved angry face. "Outside!"

They obeyed. Hal's tall body was still numb from sleep, but his mind, triggered into immediate overdrive, was whirring. He avoided looking at Jason in the interests of keeping up the pretense that they had not talked and still did not know each other, and he noticed that Jason avoided looking at him. Once in the corridor they were herded back the way Hal remembered being brought in.

"Where are we going?" Jason asked.

"Silence!" said the guard softly, without looking at him and without changing the expression of his gaunt, set features. "or I will hang thee by thy wrists for an hour or so after this is over, apostate whelp."

Jason said no more. His thin face was expressionless. His slight frame was held erect. They were moved along down several corridors, up a freight lift shaft, to what was again very obviously the office section of this establishment. Their guard brought them to join a gathering of what seemed to be twenty or more prisoners like themselves, waiting outside the open doors of a room with a raised platform at one end, a desk upon it and an open space before it. The flag of the

United Sects, a white cross on a black field, hung from a flagpole set upright on the stage.

Their guard left them with the other prisoners and stepped a few steps aside to stand with the five other guards present. They stood, guards and prisoners alike, and time went by.

Finally, there was the sound of footwear on polished corridor floor, echoing around the bend in the further corridor, and three figures turned the corner and came into sight. Hal's breath caught in his chest. Two were men in ordinary business suits—almost certainly local officials. But the man between them, tall above them, was Nigel Blas.

Nigel ran his glance over all the prisoners as he approached; and his eye paused for a second on Hal, but not for longer than might have been expected from the fact that Hal was noticeably the tallest of the group. Nigel came on and turned into the doorway, shaking his head at the two men accompanying him as he did so.

"Foolish," he was saying to them as he passed within arm's length of Hal, "Foolish, foolish! Did you think I was the sort to be impressed by what you could sweep off the streets, that I was to be amused like some primitive ruler by state executions or public torture-spectacles? This sort of thing only wastes energy. I'll show you how to do things. Bring them in here."

The guards were already moving in response before one of the men with Nigel turned and gestured at the prisoners. Hal and the others were herded into the room and lined up in three ranks facing the platform on which the two men now stood behind the desk and Nigel himself half-sat, half-lounged, with his weight on the further edge of that piece of furniture. To even this casual pose he lent an impression of elegant authority.

The sick coldness had returned to the pit of Hal's stomach with Nigel's appearance; and now that feeling was growing, spreading all through him. Sheltered and protected as he had been all his life, he had grown up without ever knowing the kind of fear that compresses the chest and takes the strength from the limbs. Then, all at once, he had encountered death and that kind of fear for the first time, all in one moment; and now the reflex set up by that moment had been triggered by a second encounter of the tall, commanding figure on the platform before him.

He was not afraid of the Friendly authorities who were holding him captive. His mind recognized the fact that they were only human, and he had deeply absorbed the principle that for any problem involving human interaction there should be a practical solution. But the sight of Nigel faced him with something that had destroyed the very pillars of his universe. He felt the paralysis of his fear staining all through him; and the rational part of him recognized that once it had taken him over completely he would throw himself upon the fate that would follow Nigel's identification of him—just to get it over with.

He reached for help, and the ghosts of three old men came out of his memory in response.

"He is no more than a weed that flourishes for a single summer's day, this man you face," said the harsh voice of Obadiah in his mind. "No more than the rain on the mountainside, blowing for a moment past the rock. God is that rock, and eternal. The rain passes and is as if it never was. Hold to the rock and ignore the rain."

"He can do nothing," said the soft voice of Walter Inteacher, "that I've not shown you at one time or another. He is only a user of skills developed by other men and women, many of whom could use them far better than he. Remember that no one's mind and body are ever more than human. Forget the fact that he is older and more experienced than you; concentrate only on a true image of what he is, and what his limits are."

"Fear is only another weapon," said Malachi, "no more dangerous in itself than a sharpened blade is. Treat it as you would any weapon. When it approaches, turn yourself to let it pass you by, then take and control the hand that guides it at you. The weapon without the hand is only one more thing—in a universe full of things."

Up on the platform Nigel looked at them all.

"Pay attention to me, my friends," he said softly. "Look at me."

They looked, Hal with the rest of them. He saw Nigel's lean, aristocratic face and pleasant brown eyes. Then, as he looked at them, those eyes began to expand until they would entirely fill his field of vision.

Reflexively, out of his training under Walter the Inteacher, he took a step back within his own mind, putting what he saw at arm's length—and all at once it was as if he was aware of things on two levels. There was the level on which he stood with the other prisoners, held by Nigel like animals transfixed by a bright light in darkness; and there was the level in which he was aware of the assault that was being made on his free will by what was hidden behind that bright light, and on which he struggled to resist it.

He thought of rock. In his mind he formed the image of a mountainside, cut and carved into an altar on which an eternal light burned. Rock and light . . . untouchable, eternal.

"I must apologize to you, my friends and brothers,"

Nigel was saying gently to all of them. "Mistakenly, you've been made to suffer; and that shouldn't be. But it was a natural mistake and small mistakes of your own have contributed to it. Examine your conscience. Is there one of you here who isn't aware of things you know you shouldn't have done . . ."

Like mist, the beginnings of rain blew upon the light and the altar. But the light continued to burn, and the rock was unchanged. Nigel's voice continued; and the rain thickened, blowing more fiercely upon the rock and the light. On the mountainside the day darkened, but the light burned on through the darkness, showing the rock still there, still unmarked and unmoved . . .

Nigel was softly showing them all the way to a worthier and happier life, a way that trusted in what he was telling them. All that they needed to do was to acknowledge the errors of their past and let themselves be guided in the proper path in the future. His words made a warm and friendly shelter away from all storm, its door open and waiting for all of them. But, sadly, Hal must remain behind, alone, out on the mountainside in the icy and violent rain, clinging to the rock so that the wind would not blow him away; with only the pure but heatless light burning in the darkness to comfort him.

Slowly, he became aware that the increasing wind had ceased growing stronger, that the rain which had been falling ever heavier was now steady, that the darkness could grow no darker—and he, the rock and the light were still there, still together. A warmth of a new sort kindled itself inside him and grew until it shouted in triumph. He felt a strength within him that he had never felt before, and with that strength, he stepped back, merging once more the two levels, so that he looked out nakedly through his own eyes again at Nigel.

Nigel had finished talking and was stepping down from the platform, headed out of the room. All the prisoners turned to watch him go as if he walked out of the room holding one string to which all of them were attached.

"If you'll come this way, brothers," said one of the guards.

They were led, by this single guard only, down more corridors and into a room with desks, where they were handed back their papers.

* * *

Apparently, they were free to go. They were ushered out of the building and Hal found himself walking down the street with Jason at his side. He looked at the other man and saw him smiling and animated.

"Howard!" Jason said. "Isn't this wonderful? We've got to find the others and tell them about this great man. They'll have to see him for themselves."

Hal looked closely into Jason's eyes.

"What is it, brother?" said Jason. "Is something wrong?"

"No," said Hal. "But maybe we should sit down somewhere and make some plans. Is there any place around here where we can talk, away from people?"

Jason looked around. They were in what appeared to Hal to be a semi-industrial section. It was mid-morning, and the rain that had been falling when they had landed the day before was now holding off, although the sky was dark and promised more precipitation.

"This early . . ." Jason hesitated. "There's a small eating place with booths in its back room, and this time of day the back room ought to be completely empty."

"Let's go," said Hal.

The eating place turned out to be small indeed. It was hardly the sort of establishment that Hal would have found himself turning into if he had simply wanted a meal, but its front room held only one group of four and one or two customers at the square tables there; and the back room, as Jason had predicted, was empty. They took a booth in a corner and ordered coffee.

"What plans did you have in mind to make, Howard?" asked Jason, when the coffee had been brought.

Hal tasted what was in his cup, and set the cup down again. Coffee—or rather some imitation of it—was to be found on all the inhabited worlds. But its taste varied largely on any two worlds, and was often markedly different in widely distant parts of the same world. Hal had spent three years getting used to Coby coffee. He would have to start all over again with Harmony coffee.

"Have you seen this?" he asked, in turn.

From a pocket he brought out a small gold nugget encased in a cube of glass. It was the first piece of pocket gold he had found in the Yow Dee Mine; and, following a Coby custom, he had bought it back from the mine owners and had it encased in glass, to carry about as a good-luck piece. His fellow team-members would have thought him strange if he had not. Now, for the first time, he had a use for it.

Jason bent over the cube.

"Is that real gold?" he asked, with the fascination of anyone not of either Coby or Earth.

"Yes," said Hal. "See the color . . ."

He reached out across the table and took the back of Jason's neck gently and precisely between the tips of his thumb and middle finger. The skin beneath his fingertips jumped at his touch, then relaxed as he put soft pressure on the nerve endings below it.

"Easy," he said, "just watch the piece of gold . . . Jason, I want you to rest for a bit. Just close your eyes and lean back against the back of the booth and sleep for a couple of minutes. Then you can open your eyes and listen. I've got something to tell you."

With an obedience a little too ready to be natural, Jason closed his eyes and leaned back, resting his head against the hard, dark-dyed wooden panel that was the back of the booth. Hal took his hand from the other's neck and Jason stayed as he was, breathing easily and deeply for about a hundred and fifty heart-beats. Then he opened his eyes and stared at Hal as if puzzled for a second. He smiled.

"You were going to tell me something," he said.

"Yes," said Hal. "And you're going to listen to me all the way through and then not say anything until you've thought about what I've just told you. Aren't you?"

"Yes, Howard," said Jason.

"Good. Now listen closely." Hal paused. He had never done anything like this before; and there was a danger, in Jason's present unnaturally receptive state, that some words Hal used might have a larger effect than he had intended it to have. "Because I want you to understand something. Right now you think you're acting normally and doing exactly what you'd ordinarily want to do. But actually, that's not the case. The fact is, a very powerful individual's made you an attractive offer on a level where it's hard for you to refuse him, a choice to let your conscience go to sleep and leave all moral decisions up to someone else. Because you were approached on that particular level, you've no way of judging whether this was a wise decision to make, or not. Do you follow me so far? Nod your head if you do."

Jason nodded. He was concentrating just hard enough to bring a small frown line into being between his eyebrows. But otherwise his face was still relaxed and happy.

"Essentially what you've just been told," Hal said, "is that Nigel Blas, or people designated by him, will decide not only what's right for you, but what you'll want to do; and you've agreed that this would be a good thing. Because of that, you've now joined those who've already made that agreement with him; those who were until an hour ago your enemies, in that they were trying to destroy the faith you've held to all your life . . ."

The slight frown was deepening between Jason's brows and the happiness on his face was being replaced by a strained expression. Hal talked on; and when at last he stopped, Jason was huddled on the other seat, turned as far away from Hal as the close confines of the booth would allow, with his face hidden in his hands.

Hal sat, feeling miserable himself, and tried to drink his coffee. The silence between them continued, until finally Jason heaved a long, shivering sigh and dropped his hands. He turned a face to Hal that looked as if it had not slept for two nights.

"Oh, God!" he said.

Hal looked back at him, but did not try to say anything.

"I'm unclean," said Jason. "Unclean!"

"Nonsense," said Hal. Jason's eyes jumped to his face; and Hal made himself grin at the other. "What was that I seem to remember hearing when I was

young—and you must've remembered hearing, too—
about the sin of pride? What makes you feel you're
particularly evil in having knuckled under to the persuasion of Nigel Blas?"

"I lacked faith!" said Jason.

"We all lack faith to some extent," Hal said. "There
are probably some men and women so strong in their
faith that Blas wouldn't have been able to touch them.
I had a teacher once . . . but the point is, everyone else
in that room gave in to him, the same way you did."

"You didn't."

"I've had special training," said Hal. "That's what
I was telling you just now, remember? What Nigel
Blas did, he succeeded in doing because he's also had
special training. Believe me, someone without training
would have had to have been a very remarkable person
to resist him. But for someone with training, it was . . .
relatively easy."

Jason drew another deep, ragged breath.

"Then I'm ashamed for another reason," he said
bleakly.

"Why?" Hal stared at him.

"Because I thought you were a spy, planted on me
by the Accursed of God, when they decided to hold me
captive. When we heard Howard Immanuelson had
died of a lung disease in a holding station on Coby, we
all assumed his papers had been lost. The thought that
someone else of the faith could find them and use them
—and his doing it would be so secret that someone like
myself wouldn't know—that was stretching coin-
cidence beyond belief. And you were so quick to pick
up the finger speech. So I was going to pretend I was
taken in by you. I was going to bring you with me to
some place where the other brothers and sisters of the
faith could question you and find out why you were

sent and what you knew about us."

He stared burningly at Hal.

"And then you, just now, brought me back from Hell—from where I could never have come back without you. There was no need for you to do that if you had been one of the enemy, one of the Accursed. How could I have doubted that you were of the faith?"

"Quite easily," said Hal. "As far as bringing you back from Hell, all I did was hurry up the process a little. The kind of persuasion Nigel Blas was using only takes permanently with people who basically agree with him to begin with. With those who don't, his type of mind-changing gets eaten away by the natural feelings of the individual until it wears thin and breaks down. Since you were someone opposed enough to him to fight him, the only way he could stop you permanently would be to kill you."

"Why didn't he then?" said Jason. "Why didn't he kill all of us?"

"Because it's to his advantage to pretend that he only opens people's eyes to the right way to live," said Hal, hearing an echo of Walter the Inteacher in the words even as he said them. He had not consciously stopped to think the matter out, but Jason's question had automatically evoked the obvious answer. "Even his convinced followers feel safer if he is always right, always merciful. What he did with us, there, wasn't because we were important, but because the two men with him on the platform were important—to him. There're really only a handful of what you call the Belial-spawn, compared to the trillions of people on the fourteen worlds. Those like Nigel don't have the time, even if they felt like it, to control everyone personally. So, whenever possible they use the same sort of social mechanisms that've been used down the centuries when a few people wanted to command many."

Jason sat watching him.

"Who are you, Howard?" he asked.

"I'm sorry." Hal hesitated. "I can't tell you that. But I should tell you you've no obligation to call me brother. I'm afraid I lied to you. I'm not of the faith, as you call it. I've got nothing to do with whatever organization you and those with you belong to. But I am at war with Nigel Blas and his kind."

"Then you're a brother," said Jason, simply. He picked up his own cold coffee cup and drank deeply from it. "We—those the Accursed call the Children— are of every sect and every possible interpretation of the Idea of God. Your difference from the rest of us isn't any greater than our differences from each other. But I'm glad you told me this, because I'll have to tell the others about you when we reach them."

"Can we reach them?" asked Hal.

"There's no problem about that," said Jason. "I'll make contact in town here with someone who'll know where the closest band of warriors is, right now; and we'll join them. Out in the countryside we of the faith still control. Oh, they chase us, but they can't do more than keep us on the move. It's only here, in the cities, that the Belial-spawn and their minions rule."

He slid to the end of the booth and stood up.

"Come along," he said.

Out in the coldly damp air of the street, they located a callbox and coded for an autocab. In succession, they visited a clothing store, a library and a gymnasium, without Jason's recognizing anyone he trusted enough to ask for help. Their fourth try brought them to a small vehicle custom-repair garage in the northern outskirts of Citadel.

The garage itself was a dome-like temporary structure perched in an open field out where residences gave way to small personal farm-plots rented by city dwellers on an annual basis. It occupied an open stretch of stony ground that was its own best demonstration of why it had not been put to personal farming the way the land around it had. Inside the barely-heated dome, the air of which was thick with the faintly banana-like smell of a local tree oil used for lubrication hanging like an invisible mist over the half-dismantled engines of several surface vehicles, they found a single occupant—a square, short, leathery man in his sixties, engaged in reassembling the rear support fan of an all-terrain fourplace cruiser.

"Hilary!" said Jason, as they reached him.

"Jase—" said the worker, barely glancing up at them. "When did you get back?"

"Yesterday," said Jason. "The Accursed put us up overnight in their special hotel. This is Howard Immanuelson. Not of the faith, but one of our allies. From Coby."

"Coby?" Hilary glanced up once more at Hal. "What did you do on Coby?"

"I was a miner," said Hal.

Hilary reached for a cleansing rag, wiped his hands, turned about and offered one of them to Hal.

"Long?" he asked.

"Three years."

Hilary nodded.

"I like people who know how to work," he said. "You two on the run?"

"No," said Jason. "They turned us loose. But we need to get out into the country. Who's close right now?"

Hilary looked down at his hands and wiped them once more on his cloth, then threw the cloth in a wastebin.

"Rukh Tamani," he said. "She and her people're passing through, on their way to something. You know Rukh?"

"I know of her," said Jason. "She's a sword of the Lord."

"You might connect up with them. Want me to give you a map?"

"Please," said Jason. "And if you can supply us—"

"Clothes and gear, that's all," said Hilary. "Weapons are getting too risky."

"Can you take us close to her, at all?"

"Oh, I can get you fairly well in." Hilary looked again at Hal. "Anything I'll be able to give you in the way of clothes is going to fit pretty tight."

"Let's try what you've got," said Jason.

Hilary led them to a partitioned-off corner of his dome. The door they went through let them into a storeroom piled to the ceiling with a jumble of containers and goods of all kinds. Hilary threaded his way among the stacks to a pile of what seemed to be mainly clothing and camping gear, and started pulling out items.

Twenty minutes later, he had them both outfitted with heavy bush clothing including both shoulder and belt packs and camping equipment. As Hilary had predicted, Hal's shirt, jacket and undershirt were tight in the shoulders and short in the sleeves. Otherwise, everything that he had given Hal fitted well enough. The one particular blessing turned out to be the fact that there were bush boots available of the proper length for Hal's feet. They were a little too wide, but extra socks and insoles took care of that.

"Now," Hilary said when the outfitting was complete. "When did you eat last?"

Hunger returned to Hal's consciousness like a body blow. Unconsciously, once it had become obvious in the cell that there was no hope of food soon, he had blocked out his need for it—strongly enough that he had even sat in the coffee place with Jason and not thought of food, when he could have had it for the ordering. As it was, Jason answered before he did.

"We didn't. Not since we got off the ship."

"Then I better feed you, hadn't I?" grunted Hilary. He led them out of the storeroom and into another corner of the dome that had a cot, sink, foodkeeper and cooking equipment.

He fed them an enormous meal, mainly of fried vegetables, local mutton and bread, washed down with quantities of a flat, semi-sweet root beer, apparently made from a variform of the native Earth product. The heavy intake of food operated on Hal like a sedative. Once they had all piled into a battered six-place bush van, he stretched out and fell asleep.

He woke to a rhythmic sound that was the slashing of branch tips against the sides of the van. Looking out the windows on either side, he saw that they were proceeding down a forest track so narrow that the bushes on either side barely allowed the van to pass. Jason and Hilary were in mid-conversation in the front seat of the van.

". . . Of course it won't stop them!" Hilary was saying. "But if there's anything at all the Belial-spawn are even a little sensitive to, it's public opinion. If Rukh and her people can take care of the core shaft tap, it'll be a choice for them of starving Hope, Valleyvale, and the other local cities, or shifting the ship outfitting to the core tap center on South Promise. It'll save them trouble to shift. It's a temporary spoke in their wheel, that's all; but what more can we ask?"

"We can ask to win," said Jason.

"God allowed the spawn to gain control in our cities," said Hilary. "In His time, He will release us from them. Until then, our job is to testify for Him by doing all we can to resist them."

Jason sighed.

"Hilary," he said. "Sometimes I forget you're just like the other old folk when it comes to anything that looks like an act of God's will."

"You haven't lived long enough yet," Hilary said. "To you, everything seems to turn on what's happened in your own few years. Get older and look around the fourteen worlds, and you'll see that the time of Judgement's not that far off. Our race is old and sick in sin. On every world, things are falling into disorder and decay, and the coming among us of these mixed breeds who'd make everyone else into their personal cattle is only one more sign of the approach of Judgement."

"I can't take that attitude," said Jason, shaking his head. "We wouldn't be capable of hope, if hope had no meaning."

"It's got meaning," said Hilary, "in a practical sense. Forcing the spawn to change their plans to another core tap delays them; and who's to know but that very delay may be part of the battle plan of the Lord, as he girds his loins to fight this last and greatest fight?"

The noise of the branches hitting the sides and windows of the van ceased suddenly. They had emerged into an open area overgrown only by tall, straight-limbed conifers—variforms of some Earthly stock—spaced about upon uneven, rocky ground that had hardly any covering beyond patches of green moss and brown, dead needles fallen from the trees. The sun, for the first time Hal had seen it since he had arrived on Harmony, was breaking through a high-lying mass of white and black clouds, wind-torn here and there to show occasional patches of startling blue and brilliant light. The ground-level breeze blew strongly against the van; and for the first time Hal became aware that their way was uphill. With that recognition, the realization came that the plant life and the terrain indicated a considerably higher altitude than that of Citadel.

Hal sat up on the seat.

"You alive back there?" said Hilary.

"Yes," answered Hal.

"We'll be there in a few minutes, Howard," said Jason. "Let me talk to Rukh about you, first. It'll be her decision as to whether you're allowed to join her group, or not. If she won't have you, I'll come back with you, too; and we'll stay together until Hilary can find a group that'll have us both."

"You'll be on your own, if I have to take you back," said Hilary. "I can't afford to keep you around my place for fear of attracting attention."

"We know that," said Jason.

The van went up and over a rise of the terrain, and nosed down abruptly into a valley-like depression that was like a knife-cut in the slope. Some ten or twenty meters below was the bed of the valley, with a small stream running through it; the stream itself was hardly visible because of the thick cluster of small trees that grew about its moisture. The van slid down the slope of the valley wall on the air-cushion of its fans, plunged in among the trees, and came to a halt at a short distance from the near edge of the stream. From above, Hal had seen nothing of people or shelters, but suddenly they were in the midst of a small encampment.

He took it in at one glance. It was a picture that was to stay in his mind afterwards. Brightly touched by a moment of the sunlight breaking through the ragged clouds overhead, he saw a number of collapsible shelters like beehives the height of a grown man, their olive-colored side panels and tops further camouflaged by tree branches fastened about them. Two men were standing in the stream, apparently washing clothes. A woman approaching middle age, in a black, leather-like jacket, was just coming out of the trees to the left of the van. On a rock in the center of the clearing sat a gray-haired man with a cone rifle half torn down for cleaning its parts, lying on a cloth he had spread across his knees. Facing him, and turning now to face the van, was a tall, slim, dark young woman in a somber green bush jacket, its large number of square pockets bulging with their contents. Below the bush jacket, she wore heavy bush pants tucked into the tops of short boots. A gunbelt and sidearm were hooked tightly about her narrow waist, the black holster holding the sidearm with its weather flap clipped firmly down.

She wore nothing on her head. Her black hair was cut short about her ears, and her face was narrow and perfect below a wide brow and brilliant, dark eyes. In that single, arrested moment, the repressed poet in Hal woke, and he thought that she was like the dark blade of a sword in the sunlight. Then his attention was jerked from her. In a series of flashing motions the disassembled parts of the cone rifle in the hands of the gray-haired man were thrown back together, ending with the hard slap of a new tube of cones into the magazine slot below the barrel. The man was almost as swift as Hal had seen Malachi be in similar demonstrations. The movements of this man did not have the smooth, unitary flow of Malachi's—but he was almost as fast.

"All right," said the woman in the bush jacket. "It's Hilary."

The hands of the gray-haired man relaxed on the now-ready weapon; but the weapon itself still lay on the cloth over his knees, pointing in the general direction of Hal and the other two. Hilary got out of the van. Jason and Hal did the same.

"I brought you a couple of recruits," said Hilary, as coolly as if the man on the rock was holding a stick of candy. He started to walk forward and Jason moved after him. Hal followed.

"This is Jason Rowe," said Hilary. "Maybe you know him. The other's not of the faith, but a friend. He's Howard Immanuelson, a miner from Coby."

By the time he had finished saying this he was within a meter and a half of the woman and the man with Jason and Hal a step behind. Hilary stopped. The woman glanced at Jason, nodded briefly, then turned her brilliant gaze on Hal.

"Immanuelson?" she said. "I'm Rukh Tamani. This is my sergeant, James Child-of-God."

Hal found it hard to look away from her, but he turned his gaze on the face of the gray-haired man. He found himself looking into a rectangular, raw-boned set of features, clothed in skin gone leathery some years since from sun and weather. Lines radiated from the corners of the eyes of James Child-of-God; deeper lines had carved themselves in long curves about the corners of his mouth, from nose to chin, and the pale blue eyes he fastened on Hal were like the muzzles of cone rifles.

"If not of the faith," he said to them all now, in a dry, penetrating tenor voice, "he hath no right here among us."

BESTSELLING
Science Fiction
and
Fantasy

☐ 47810-7	**THE LEFT HAND OF DARKNESS,** Ursula K. Le Guin	$2.95
☐ 16021-2	**DORSAI!,** Gordon R. Dickson	$2.95
☐ 80583-3	**THIEVES' WORLD,**™ Robert Lynn Asprin, editor	$2.95
☐ 11456-3	**CONAN #1,** Robert E. Howard, L. Sprague de Camp, Lin Carter	$2.75
☐ 49142-1	**LORD DARCY INVESTIGATES,** Randall Garrett	$2.75
☐ 21889-X	**EXPANDED UNIVERSE,** Robert A. Heinlein	$3.95
☐ 87330-8	**THE WARLOCK UNLOCKED,** Christopher Stasheff	$2.95
☐ 10264-6	**CHANGELING,** Roger Zelazny	$2.95
☐ 51553-3	**THE MAGIC GOES AWAY,** Larry Niven	$2.95

Prices may be slightly higher in Canada.